THE NICE QUIET GIRL

By the same author:

The Hunting of Mr. Gloves

As "Peter Chambers":

The Day the Thames Caught Fire

THE NICE QUIET GIRL

by

PHILIP DANIELS

St. Martin's Press
New York

Library of Congress Cataloging-in-Publication Data

Daniels, Philip.
    The nice quiet girl / Philip Daniels.
        p.   cm.
    "A Thomas Dunne book."
    ISBN 0-312-07043-8
    I. Title.
    PR6054.A522N5   1992
    823'.914—dc20   91-34918
                                                              CIP

First published in Great Britain by Robert Hale Limited.

First U.S. Edition: January 1992
10 9 8 7 6 5 4 3 2 1

ONE

The huge eight-wheeled transport turned off the main road, into the unlit area that fronted the all-night café. The night was dark, and rain pattered gently at the driver's face as he swung open his door, and climbed the two rungs down to the ground.

He was a tall man, burly, with a red, good-natured face below a thatch of black, curly hair. Now he stretched prodigiously and yawned. One thing about Walt's, he reflected, you'd be sure of something decent to eat. Hot, too. Word got around fast among the truckies. If a man thought he'd been overcharged somewhere up North, the word would be in Bristol within a couple of days. That was enough to put a café-owner out of business, if he catered to the long-haul driving trade. Walt's was O.K.

" That you, Ed?"

He turned quickly towards the approaching voice, peering into the night.

" Oh, hello Ron. Been in, have you?"

" Yeah. Busy night. Quite a few in. Remember I told you about that curry load I was expecting? Thought we might be able to do a bit?"

" What about it?"

" My twat guvnor lost the job. It's going by train."

" Train?" echoed Ed, scornfully. " Twat guvnor is right. So we haven't got any business, then? Pity, with the holidays coming up. I could use a few extra greens."

Ron shrugged.

" So we lose a few. Something else'll turn up."

"Yeah. Talking about turning up, is the missus working in there tonight?"

Ron was mystified.

"The missus? I've been coming in here about four years, and I never laid eyes on her. What makes you ask?"

Ed looked crafty.

"I've been coming longer than that, and I've never seen her, either. But I was told she showed up the other night. Behind the counter. Bit of a darling, too, they reckon. No wonder old Walt keeps her locked up."

"Go on? Cunning sod. Well, she's not there now. I was beginning to think it was all a take-on. Perhaps Walt never had no missus at all."

"Oh, she's there all right. Like to have seen her. Perhaps I'll comb my hair. Wouldn't take much to push old Walt's nose out."

Ron chuckled.

"Still the bleeding Romeo, eh? Well, let me know how you get on. If you do get on, that is."

They both laughed, and Ron walked away to his own lorry.

Ed went across the forecourt, and up the three steps to the white-painted doors. A rush of fatty, smoke-laden air greeted him as he stepped inside. A juke box was blaring, and one of the younger drivers stood beside it, drumming with thick fingers on top of the machine. Everyone inspected the newcomer, recognised him, and got on with their own affairs.

Behind the stainless steel counter, a middle-aged man watched him approach. There was no sign of a woman, except for the faded old creature who waddled around clearing the tables.

"Ed," greeted the owner.

"Wotcher Walt. Eggs, bacon, chips, fried bread."

"Right. How many eggs?"

6

" Three."

" Give you a shout."

Ed parked himself at an empty table and took out a crumpled packet of cigarettes. Another man came over and leaned down, speaking quietly.

" Shan't be putting any curry on it this weekend."

" No," Ed shook his head. " I seen Ron outside."

" Pity. Holidays coming up."

" That's what I said."

The newcomer looked over his shoulder before speaking again.

" I hear there's a few loose hammers going about. You interested?"

Ed looked at him scornfully.

" Hammers? What would I do with bleeding hammers? You want some of the building lads."

" Yeah. Still, thought I'd mention it."

He went away. Ed pulled a tattered newspaper from under his thick jacket, and turned to page three.

" Ed."

He looked up to see Walt beckoning, and went back to the counter.

" There you go. Extra bacon tonight. One of the lads dropped me a bit. Sort of present."

" Looks all right."

Ed handed over his money, and waited for change, while Walt opened the till.

" Missed a treat then, they tell me."

" Treat?"

Walt was busy sorting coins.

" Your missus. I hear she come out to give you a hand the other night."

Walt shut the till-drawer, and came back to his customer, counting the change into his hands.

" Yeah," he confirmed. " Funny, that was. All these

years, she refused to help at the counter. Helps outside, mind you. Don't get any wrong ideas. She's not sitting indoors eating chocolates. No, she works hard, bloody hard, out in the back. But she won't come in here. Then, suddenly, the other night, she changes her mind. Only the once, mind you. That was enough. She's not been back."

"Gorn," scoffed Ed, "you're making it up. It's you keeps her locked out there. Afraid she might get swept up by one of us good-looking bastards."

Walt grinned good-naturedly.

"Can't blame me, eh? Fine looking body of men like this."

"Crafty old sod."

Ed picked up his meal and went away.

Walter Ellis picked up a cloth automatically, and wiped at a few spots of grease on the counter. He liked the counter to be immaculate. He smiled to himself at the thought of Ruby, his Ruby, with any of these roughnecks. A lady, that's what Ruby was. Why she'd ever been content to settle down with him was something he'd long ceased to ponder. A worker too, just as he'd been saying. Thinking about her reminded him that he hadn't seen her for best part of half an hour. She took a little break sometimes, if she felt like it, but not usually this long. The old woman waddled in behind him with a fresh stack of plates.

"Missus out there, Ade?"

"No, Mr. Ellis. Ain't seen her for ever such a long time."

Old cow. Always exaggerating the amount of work she did. That, together with the endless nightly recital of her ailments, made Ellis wonder why he kept her on. But he knew the answer, really. Old Ade needed the job, and nobody else in Great Fording would employ her. Or could, for that matter. It wasn't exactly what you'd call an industrial estate. Just a few dozen houses, one church, three pubs,

8

and a general store cum post-office. Not much scope for an old woman with bad legs.

Where was Ruby, then? Perhaps she was having one of her headaches. It was Walt's habit to remove money from the till at regular intervals and take it across to the house, where there was a proper safe. An all-night café is an easy target for a quick hold-up during one of the lulls that occur in the small hours, and Walter Ellis liked to be on the safe side. Now, he looked around at his customers. All good regulars, reliable people. He wouldn't be missed for a couple of minutes.

" It's all under control, Ade," he told the old crone. " I'm just going to nip over and see Mrs. Ellis is all right."

" Right you are."

Walt left twenty pounds behind him, in notes and change, and stuffed the rest of the money into his pockets. Then he went through the small kitchen area, and out through a back door. It was only a matter of twenty yards across to the comfortable house where the Ellis family lived, and the area was brilliantly lit by overhead fluorescent tubes. Walt wasn't going to risk having any of his family attacked between the two buildings, not if a bit of lighting could stop it. The small front gate stood open, and that puzzled him. They were all very good about keeping it shut, even the kids, now they were older.

He took his keys, ready to open the front door, but as his extended hand touched it, the door swung open. He was now definitely alarmed.

" Ruby," he called, dashing inside. " Ruby."

There was no answer. He snapped down light switches, flooding the hallway.

" Ruby."

He looked first into the kitchen. Empty. Then he ran into the sitting room, then the small dining room. He went up the stairs two at a time.

9

"Ruby."

She was in the bedroom.

She lay on the bed, naked, except for a flimsy pink nightdress which was pulled up round her throat. Her flat stomach was a mass of blood, from gaping obscene wounds. Her dead face was turned sideways, and her mouth hung slackly open.

"Ruby."

A thin animal scream of disbelieving anguish ripped from his throat at the sight of her.

"Dad? What's all the—oh, Christ."

His son Matt had appeared at the doorway, pulling on a dressing-gown. Now he stood, gaping. It wasn't right. It wasn't right an eighteen year old boy should see her like that. Walt wanted to order him out, but knew it was futile.

Matt watched in horror, as his father dropped to his knees beside the dead woman, grabbing her hand and kissing it, and speaking to her, and crying. All at the same time. Didn't he know she was dead?

Dead. And horribly dead. His mind, confused at first by sleep, and then by shock, began to clear.

"Dad." He pulled at Walt's shoulder. "Dad. What happened here? What did you—? I mean—"

His voice tailed away as his father became suddenly still, and turned his head round.

"What did you say?"

"I—nothing. Dad, we have to get help. A doctor—or—"

"Yes. Yes, a doctor. Go and—no, wait."

Walt Ellis raised himself to his feet, staring down in anguish at his dead partner. Then he leaned over and began to tug at her nightdress.

"Dad, what do you think you're doing?"

Matt pulled at his arm. Walt shook him off.

"Can't have people seeing her like this. Not right. It isn't decent—"

" Dad."

The urgency in his son's tone arrested his action. Why was the boy meddling? Surely he must understand—

Matt's face was white.

" Dad, you mustn't. Mustn't touch her, dad. Ruby's been—been murdered. Don't you see? Mustn't touch her."

" Murdered?"

Even the voice didn't sound like his own. Nothing was real any more.

*   *   *

Detective-Inspector Joe Barnett stirred at his tea, and looked into the tired face of the boy at the other side of the kitchen table. Seemed like a decent enough lad, he reflected. Good thing he'd been here, too. He'd been the one who'd called in the ambulance people, and the police. Even had the sense to alert the customers in the café, and ask them to wait around until the police arrived. Not that they'd all obeyed him, but at least those who stayed made a note of the ones who pushed off. Yes, the boy had done very well. If it hadn't been for him there might have been hours of delay. The father was in no state to think clearly.

" You must be a heavy sleeper, Matt. The gun was fired four times at least. Hell of a noise."

Matthew Ellis nodded.

" I'm hard to shift, once I get to sleep. And my room is right at the far end of the landing. Don't forget, this is an all-night café. I was only eight when we started here. You have to learn how to stay asleep, what with lorry doors banging, and those big engines roaring all the time." He grinned slightly. " I think I could sleep through a war."

The policeman doubted it. He'd heard war. Not many people stayed asleep.

" Your father mentioned your sister, earlier on. Where is she now?"

" Bristol. She's at the university. Post-graduate course, one year."

" Ah. She already has her degree, then?"

" Oh yes," and there was pride in the boy's tone. " First class honours. Iris is nearly twenty-two."

The inspector sipped at his almost-black tea. Pity to have to be talking to an eighteen year old about the situation, but there was no alternative. The father was in a state of mild shock, and there were no relatives in the village. The girl would be needed here.

" She'll have to be told, you know," he said gently. " Better coming from you, than having a uniformed officer breaking the news."

Matt bowed his head, and his voice was low.

" Yes. She told me she gets up about half past seven. I'll ring her then."

" If she can get home for a few days, so much the better," Barnett advised. " Lot to be cleared up. Your step-mother's clothes. That sort of thing."

The young man nodded, without replying. A man in a dark blue suit looked round the kitchen door.

" We're all done upstairs," he announced.

" Right. Can the victim be moved now?"

" Doctor would like a word, first." The newcomer looked at the son of the house, choosing his words. " He's waiting in the sitting room. Thought you might be too busy in here."

Barnett clicked his teeth, standing up.

" I'll come right away. Before I go, Matt, tell me one thing. When did you first notice the safe was open?"

" Safe?' Matthew's brow clouded, as he transferred his thoughts to this new problem. " Oh. Er—well, I don't really know. I only really saw Ruby, you see."

" Yes, naturally. But do you think it was before you called us, or afterwards?"

Silly bloody question. What difference could it possibly make when he first noticed it? The thing was open, wasn't it? Whether he noticed it or not.

"Well, then, I suppose it was after. After I made the calls. I went back up—up there—to try to get my father to leave her. There was nothing he could do, you see, and I thought he'd be better off down here with me."

"But he wouldn't come?"

"No. It wasn't until the sergeant—you know, the one who got here first—it wasn't till he practically ordered dad out of the bedroom, that he would leave her alone."

"Understandable," said Barnett comfortably. "They were very close, I believe?"

"Yes. She's wonderful, I mean, she was—I mean—"

Large tears formed in Matt's eyes, brimmed over, and tumbled unheeded down his face. The inspector had a son of about the same age, and his sympathy was not entirely professional.

"Right then, Matt. Thank you for the tea. How about putting another kettle on? I expect those technical chaps of ours would appreciate a cup before they go. Cold night outside. Morning, rather."

The boy rose automatically, and began to fill a kettle. Barnett left him and went out to the sitting room. The duty doctor was young, well under thirty, and Barnett hoped there was sufficient experience under the curly fair hair.

"What do you make of it, doctor?" he greeted.

"Gunshot wounds. Four, all fired at short range. There are actual burn marks in one case."

"That close? M'm. Anything on the weapon?"

"Heavyish to heavy. Not smaller than a point three eight, I would say. But you'll need ballistics on that one."

"Other injuries?"

"Blue welt on the upper left cheek. Not very pronounced. More the kind of thing you'd get from a hard handslap, than from being struck with a weapon."

" Right. The nightdress bothers me. Pulled up like that. Was there any sign of sexual intercourse?"

" Not at the time of death, no. I shall need to spend more time with the body to give you details of what might have happened earlier."

" Please do, doctor. Funny business. Say we have an intruder. He's busy opening the bedroom safe, when in comes Mrs. Ellis. What does he do? Nine times out of ten, he threatens her. At the most, he'll hit her over the head, to shut her up. In a real panic, his gun might go off. But this wasn't like that. He made her pull up her nightgown and then shot her in the stomach. Four times. It isn't normal at all."

" A weirdo? She was a very handsome woman. Almost beautiful, I would have judged."

Barnett nodded thoughtfully.

" A kinky thief?" he observed. " Well, it's not impossible. Nothing is impossible doctor, I'll give you that. But whoever opened that safe, knows his safes. It's an elementary job. Enough to baffle the average man, but child's play to the expert. And there's another oddity. A safe-man, peterman as we call him, he doesn't carry a gun. He's not a thug."

" Four bullet wounds in the stomach and chest," chided the doctor.

" I know. It seems to contradict me. But I stand by what I said. The peterman does not carry a gun. There's such a thing as murder by accident. Or there is in my book. What I mean is, when someone gets killed because they disturb a criminal, or they're trying to prevent him from getting away. They get killed, not because of who they are, but simply because they're in the way. Do you follow me?"

" Vaguely, yes."

" Well now, take this situation. Middle of the night.

14

Chap breaking into a safe. What for? Two hundred pounds? Three hundred? Mrs. Ellis comes in, unexpectedly. One woman. Not even dressed. What would you do? Hit her on the head? Tie her up? So would anybody else. But not our man. He murders her. Not in a panic, but in cold blood. He even made her lift up her nightdress first. Now that, doctor, is personal. That's what a man might do to his own wife, his girlfriend, someone he knows very well. Not to a stranger. Not when he came here to rob a safe. Do you begin to follow me now?"

The young doctor smiled slightly.

"Yes, I do, indeed. But surely, to follow your own reasoning, it would mean that the killing was intentional? In other words, that the killer knew the victim?"

The inspector sighed.

"Seems likely. And what was she doing here, anyway? Supposed to be at work in the café. It was only because she'd been missing for half an hour that the husband came looking for her."

"She'd just had a bath," replied the doctor.

The policeman's eyes gleamed.

"Ah. You're sure?"

"Quite sure. Apart from everything else, I went to wash my own hands after I'd examined her. There was no hot water, which suggests that Mrs. Ellis had emptied the tank, and it hadn't had enough time to reheat."

Barnett grinned.

"If you should ever feel like swapping jobs, I could get you a probationary period as a D.C."

"Thanks very much."

"One thing, before you go, doctor. Will you run tests on their hands? The father and the boy. Just to eliminate them. If the gun was held that close there ought to be powder traces."

"They won't like it."

" I know. But do it, anyway. If you please. And thank you for all the help. Can you write it all up by tomorrow?"

" You'll have it by lunchtime."

The inspector followed him out of the room. It was going to be a long, hard day, he reflected.

He began to climb the stairs.

TWO

The attractive young W.P.C. tapped at the door of the great man's office, smoothed at the front of her tunic blouse, and went in. It had long been the office policy that the best-looking woman officer on duty would take in the coffee.

Detective Superintendent Robin Morgan glowered across the room at the intruder.

" Coffee, sir."

She walked smartly to his desk, placing the flower-patterned cup and saucer carefully beside him. As she turned to go, he said:

" Just a minute."

He bent his head and sniffed.

" That's instant," he accused.

" It's the most expensive—" she began.

" Instant," he repeated. " Why haven't I got my proper coffee?"

" The percolator isn't back yet, sir."

" I see. Let us cast our minds back. How long has it been gone, now? Six months? A year?"

" I'm not really sure, sir. Quite a few weeks, I think."

"Weeks?" he boomed. "It's months. Months. It only wants a simple repair. Perhaps I'm asking too much. Do you think I'm asking too much?"

"No, sir."

"How long do you imagine I would last in this job, if it took me as long to catch thieves as it takes those layabouts to repair coffee pots? How long, eh?"

"Not very long sir, I shouldn't think."

"Damned right. Is Sergeant Horton out there?"

"Yes, sir."

"Right. Well now, you tell him this. You tell him that Mr. Morgan is not happy. Mr. Morgan finds it a very lonely situation being unhappy all by himself. Mr. Morgan had better have proper coffee tomorrow, or he's going to make a few other people unhappy. So that we can all be together. More chummy like that. You understand me, officer?"

"Oh yes, sir."

"Right. That's all."

The girl escaped, thankfully. She'd got off lightly, really, she reflected. As she pulled the door to, she saw the familiar figure of Detective Inspector Barnett approaching.

"Morning, Polly. How's he feeling today?"

"Morning, Mr. Barnett. Let's put it this way. I've just taken him his coffee. It's instant."

"Oh, blimey. Well, thanks for warning me."

He rapped at the door, and went in.

"Morning, guvnor."

"Morning, Joe."

They inspected each other across the room. They had known one another for many years, these two. Each had a proper regard for the capability of the other, and although Cocky Morgan had narrowly beaten Barnett in the promotion race, there was no lingering animosity. Barnett had been disappointed, which was natural enough, but he wasn't the type to nurse resentment. At least he'd been beaten by an honest working copper, and not some fancy pants with a lot of County influence.

" Want some coffee? It's instant."

Barnett caught the sour inflection in the last words, and grinned.

" No thanks. I've just had some tea."

" Right. Well, pull up a chair and tell me what you've got."

The visitor dragged a chair opposite the desk, sat down, and unzipped his leather case. Then he set out his papers neatly in front of him.

" The victim was Ruby Ellis, aged thirty-two, married. She and her husband Walter run Walt's Café, the all-night place at Great Fording."

" I know it."

" Right. Then you'll know that the house lies behind the café, well off the main road. What I mean is, you have to drive into the café forecourt, then around the back, to reach the house."

" Go on."

" Mrs. Ellis does most of the kitchen work. She doesn't serve in the place. This means that her husband can't be certain all the time whether she's there or not. But if she takes a break, she usually tells him, and it's seldom longer than about fifteen minutes. Last night, he noticed she'd been gone about half an hour. This worried him, because he thought perhaps she wasn't feeling well, or something. He went to look for her. She was dead in the bedroom. Four gunshot wounds in the front of the body. She was naked, except for a nightdress which was pulled up in front."

" Time?"

" About ten to three—"

" About?" Morgan's voice was sharp.

Barnett was unperturbed.

18

"We can't be absolutely accurate. Walter Ellis wasn't making a note of his movements, and he was certainly in no condition to think of checking the time when he discovered the body."

"All right. Go on."

"There's a son, Matthew, aged eighteen. He woke up when he heard his father shouting. When he saw what had happened, he dialled 999, and brought us in."

Morgan held up a finger.

"Just a minute. You say the boy woke up when his father shouted. Why didn't he wake up when the gun went off?"

"He's used to sleeping through night noises. Lived at the café since he was a small boy. I think his ears would tune out the gunshots. Put them in the same category as back-fires, which of course happen all the time. His father's voice would be an unusual sound, discordant. It's only my own theory, but I think it makes sense."

The superintendent pursed his lips doubtfully.

"H'm. Well, I won't interrupt."

"The safe had been opened, and there's cash missing. About three hundred and ten pounds, as near as we can get it. When I say opened, I mean exactly that. Not jimmied."

Morgan gave a low whistle.

"Not a very promising set-up is it? An all-night café with people wandering in and out at all hours. Might as well be a big railway station in the rush hour. What about the customers? Did anyone hear the shots, or notice anything?"

Barnett shook his head.

"Not the ones we've spoken to. Some of them had driven off, but I think we have all the names. We'll have contacted them all within the next twenty four hours."

"Anything there? I mean, the long-distance crowd are

not all bosom pals with coppers, are they? Probably wouldn't tell us much, even if they could."

" I think they might, with this one. They all seem to think well of Ellis."

" And his missus?"

The inspector made a deprecating movement with his hands.

" They don't know her. As I say, she always worked behind the scenes. It was only about a week ago that she showed up at the counter for the first time. Caused quite a stir, they tell me. She was a fine-looking woman, no doubt about that."

" Was she, now? Anything there? Bit of nonsense on the side?"

" Could be. Always possible when a man has a younger wife. And even more so when the wife looks like Ruby Ellis. I shall be having that looked into very thoroughly. Great Fording is only two pints of bitter and a bus stop. About as much chance of keeping a secret there as a snow-ball has in hell."

The superintendent removed a silver pencil from an inside pocket and began to twiddle it round in his fingers. Barnett recognised an old habit, which his chief probably didn't even realise he had.

" You mentioned that the victim was much younger than the husband. I was beginning to wonder what a thirty two year old woman was doing, with an eighteen year old son."

" I was coming to that, sir. Ruby Ellis was the second wife. They've been married eight years. There's a step-daughter as well. Iris. University student, aged twenty two. She's away at Bristol at present. Should be on her way home this morning, I hope."

" When do we get the doctor's report?"

" He promised it for lunch-time. I can tell you now,

20

though, that there is a bruise on the upper left side of the victim's face. As though someone slapped her hard, some time before the murder."

Cocky Morgan tapped his pencil thoughtfully on the desk top.

" So what have we got? An open safe, money missing. A dead woman, who either pulled her nightdress up herself, or somebody did it for her, before killing her. If it was an intruder, and he knew how to open a safe, why would he carry a gun? Or even if he did, why kill the woman? If we allow that he lost his head, and I don't allow it yet, he managed to keep cool long enough to expose her body. Nothing very panicky about that, is there? I don't like this at all, Joe."

" Nor me."

Morgan looked at his junior narrowly.

" Well, you've been there. You've had plenty of time to think about it. What's come into your head?"

" Several answers. All wild guesses. No more, guvnor. I must make that very clear. Wild guesses."

" Go on then. Guess wildly."

" Right."

Barnett leaned back, and grasped the little finger of his left hand.

" One, the opened safe." He moved along a finger. " Two, the nightdress. For my money, these things discount a casual burglar in the first place. The man who opened that safe either knew the combination, or he was a professional."

" Or somebody told him."

" Told him what?"

" The combination, Joe, the combination," said Morgan tersely.

" Ah. Yes. Agreed. Now, let's assume he was a pro, a genuine peterman. Why should he take a risk for the kind of money he could reasonably expect to find in a place like that? And in such an isolated spot. If he was disturbed, the only escape is by the A-road. We could have both directions sealed within minutes. And then, on top of that, to commit a cold-blooded murder, with all the extra risks? No. It won't do, guvnor."

Morgan wagged his head up and down.

"I agree, on the face of it. But I hope you didn't come in here just to tell me what won't do. I'd sooner hear something that will."

"Coming to it. Now, Mrs. Ellis. She'd just had a bath. Why? Middle of the night, remember, and she was due back at work."

"True," agreed the superintendent. "But I imagine it's a hot, smelly job working in the kitchen in an all-night place. A woman, who takes a bit of pride in herself, might very well decide that a bath halfway through the night is a good idea."

"Yes. But she wouldn't put on her nightdress, would she? She'd get ready to go back to work."

"You're suggesting a boyfriend, and I agree it does look that way. But the risk would have been enormous. You just told me her husband missed her after half an hour. That's why he found the body. I haven't done much leaping about on beds lately, but I would guess Mrs. Ellis was cutting it very fine by taking that bath. Not leaving much time for the high jinks, was it? No, you'll have to talk a bit faster to sell me the boyfriend, Joe."

"Still," returned Barnett doggedly, "I'm not ruling him out. Yet."

"Let me try one on you," suggested Morgan. "Mrs. Ellis has a bath. The house is empty, except for the son, and she knows he's fast asleep. The bathroom can't be more than a few steps from the bedroom. The lady doesn't bother to put any clothes on, at all. She just walks straight into the bedroom, in the buff. Friend Peter is at the safe.

He loses his nerve, kills her. Then he can't bear to look at her, so he starts to put her nightdress on. But he only gets it as far as her shoulders. Then he panics, or something disturbs him, and he leaves her like that. What do you think?"

Barnett considered this new idea, frowning. Then he said, slowly:

"I must admit, I like it better than the boyfriend angle. I haven't got anything so far which would definitely rule that out. Let's leave that one in, then. For the moment. So we're back to friend Peter. What is an armed professional doing at an isolated café at three o'clock in the morning, or half past two rather, opening a safe with three hundred notes in it? It doesn't make sense."

A silver pencil jabbed at him.

"Not if that's what he was doing," intoned his boss.

"Eh? How do you mean?"

"You're speaking with knowledge that Peter didn't have. You know there were three hundred notes in that safe. I know it, because you told me. But Peter didn't. All he knew was he had a locked safe to open."

Barnett protested.

"But Peter's not a mug. Not a new boy. He would have a rough idea of what to expect. Within a hundred or so."

Morgan nodded his agreement.

"Money, yes. But what else might there have been? Jewellery, other valuables."

"No," denied the inspector. "Ellis was in a state, I admit, but he wouldn't have forgotten anything like that."

"Wouldn't he? What do we know about friend Ellis? Suppose there was something? Not even his own property, perhaps? Something he was looking after for a friend. Something stolen. That would make it worth Peter's while, wouldn't it? Might explain a lot."

It was all right for Cocky, reflected Barnett. Sitting there,

23

tossing out theories.

" I've asked for a routine report on Walter Ellis, as a matter of course," he replied stiffly.

Morgan picked up one of the two telephones on his desk.

" Sergeant Horton," he grunted. " Mr. Barnett asked for a check on Mr. Walter Ellis. How much longer are we going to have to wait? What? Well, bring it in, man."

He banged the instrument down, and sighed with despair.

" They've got it outside. They were waiting to give it to you, on the way out. Makes you weep, doesn't it?"

There was a knock at the door, and a worried-looking uniformed sergeant came in, carrying a slim brown file. Morgan held out his hand, grim-faced.

" Thank you so much, sergeant. Nothing else tucked away, have we? Little surprises for the inspector and me? I mean you're not keeping a nice signed confession for a birthday treat, or anything like that?"

" No sir," mumbled Horton. " Sorry sir, I didn't—"

" Try to shut the door quietly, sergeant."

The discomfited officer made his way out at a semi-run. Morgan grunted, and opened the file. Barnett wished he could read upside down. There was silence in the room. The superintendent sniffed once, and his visitor looked up hopefully, but the blue eyes kept on reading. Finally, the folder was laid open on the table between them.

Barnett waited.

" Your Mr. Ellis. Interesting man, according to this. The Regional Crime people have sent us two advising memos over the past three years. Not about him in particular, but about the café. You know as well as I do that a lot of materials and supplies go adrift in transit. Twice the Regional boys have almost been able to pinpoint the café as having been a transfer point."

"But nothing definite?"

Morgan shrugged.

"You know how easy it is. Three o'clock, four o'clock in the morning. A couple of cases, off one lorry, into another. Ten minutes' work. Less. The lorries go off in different directions. An hour later they're a hundred miles apart. Depending on how far they're going, what kind of care is taken by the shipping clerks at the receiving end, it's probably days, weeks, before any discrepancy is discovered. If ever. And, even if it is, it's nigh impossible to prove which day, which driver, which load. Still and all, the café has come under suspicion twice."

"Maybe so, but I couldn't take that as any kind of allegation against the proprietor. A quiet-living, industrious man, highly thought of in the village, not least by the local copper."

Morgan's eyes twinkled.

"Didn't stop you running a check on him."

Barnett bridled.

"I always check everybody in a murder case."

The superintendent relented.

"As well you did, Joe. What did you learn about the first Mrs. Ellis?"

"The first wife?" Barnett was surprised. "Well, almost nothing, really. I know there was an accident of some kind. But that was years ago."

Cocky Morgan pointed at the file.

"Paper has a good memory," he said solemnly. "The accident took place indoors. In the same house. They'd only just moved in at the time. Mrs. Ellis fell downstairs. She was carrying her third child. The fall killed her. Some of her injuries did not seem consistent with the kind of fall she had. Our people had a very close look at the whole thing. They didn't like it. You know the way you sometimes get a feeling when you're carrying out an investigation? Well, they had it then. A twitching of the nose. For one thing, the blood type of the unborn child revealed that Walter Ellis could not have been the father. That kept them more interested than ever. But they could never prove anything, never come up with enough to make a case. The verdict was accidental death, and that's what the record shows."

He paused, and waited for Barnett's reaction. The inspector made a low, hissing noise between his teeth.

"Well, well. So our Mr. Ellis has now lost two wives in strange circumstances. Changes the picture a bit, doesn't it?"

"It does. Somebody once said, if you lose one wife, it can be just carelessness. But to lose two, that is sheer bloody incompetence. At least, I think that's what he said."

Barnett nodded.

"I asked the doctor to do the paraffin thing on his hands. And the son's, by the way. But I don't expect results."

"No, not these days. What with these know-all crime writers, and the television, and the newspapers, even a child of ten knows he should wear gloves. Better have a look round for a pair."

"That I will. Funny thing, I asked the son, Matthew, when he first noticed the safe was open. He said the first time he could swear to was after he'd been downstairs to telephone us."

"Leaving his father alone in the bedroom?"

"Exactly. It's not conclusive, not by any means, but it could be a pointer."

"Another pointer," emphasised Morgan.

Barnett went on, almost as though he was thinking aloud.

"Opening the safe could have been a last-minute idea. To introduce the suggestion of an intruder."

"Right. And he wouldn't have anything lying around in a bedroom that he could use as a jimmy. Besides, it

26

would make a noise."

Barnett began to put his papers neatly together.

" A lot to do yet, of course. Lot of reports and information to come in. Too early to jump to conclusions."

" Absolutely agree, inspector. Everything must be gone into a great deal further. But I think, even at this stage, I ought to sound a small warning note."

Joe Barnett raised his eyebrow.

" Sir?"

" Yes. A small warning. If I get a request from you to send a signal to Interpol, asking for the movements of all known international safe-breakers over the past twenty four hours, I shall need a bit of convincing before I process it. This doesn't somehow have quite the flavour of an international crime ring, if you follow my drift."

Barnett grinned.

" Pity. I was hoping to get sent to Buenos Aires with an extradition warrant."

Morgan smiled back.

" Not this time, Joe. I think I'd be inclined to concentrate on trying to extradite Mr. Walter Ellis from behind his frying pan. Checking every other avenue thoroughly, of course."

" Of course. Well, if that's all sir, I'll get on."

He was at the door when the superintendent said irritably:

" Bugger."

" Sir?"

" Not you, Joe. Nothing."

Morgan didn't want anyone to know he'd let his coffee go cold.

THREE

Iris tapped at her brother's door.

" Can I come in, Matt?"

" It's open."

Her brother had only pulled open one half of the curtains. The effect was that half the room was in daylight, the rest in semi-darkness. Matthew Ellis lay on his bed in the gloomy area, one arm behind his propped-up head, and a cigarette glowing in the other hand.

She stepped inside, closing the door behind her, and sat in his old chair by the dressing table.

" Anything up?" he queried.

" No, I just got a bit fed up sitting downstairs by myself."

He turned his head, located the ashtray on the bedside table, and crushed out the cigarette.

" Old man asleep?"

" Yes, I finally persuaded him to take one of those pills the doctor left for him. Must be some kind of internal bomb. He went out like a light."

" Good."

Walter Ellis always worked in the café from seven p.m., when the day-people finished, until seven in the morning. Then he would have some breakfast, if he could face food after a whole night of serving it. By eight a.m. he would be in bed, and there he would remain until exactly one thirty in the afternoon. That had been the rule, for Ruby and himself, ever since the two young people could remember. Since his wife's murder, two weeks earlier, he had been unable to rest in the mornings, but still insisted on doing his full night's work. As a result he was becoming rapidly more gaunt in the face, more shuffling in his step, and a positive danger to himself with the various gas and electrical appliances in the café. Until today, he had refused to take any of the prescribed pills, so Iris had brought good news.

Matt said:

" Did you promise to wake him up at half past one?"

" Faithfully."

" Are you going to do it?"

" No. He needs the sleep."

They exchanged a smile across the room. Brother and sister were very close. When their mother had died, Iris had been twelve years old, Matthew eight. They had drawn together, the way children will in the face of tragedy, and set about the business of tackling a strange, motherless world. Their father needed their support, and this, too, they knew as by instinct. The girl assumed the role of part-time mother, but her father quickly saw the dangers of a life filled with cooking, washing and household chores. His daughter was not going to be denied the right to a life of her own, not if he could do anything to prevent it. And so, there was a procession of housekeepers. For various reasons, they were all unsuitable. Some were lazy, some incompetent, some too hard on the children. But the most commonly-found fault was their assumption that a vigorous man like Walter Ellis needed them in his bed. He was always surprised and upset when this development occurred. In his mind, the position was quite clear. If a man advertises for a housekeeper, he does so as an employer. If he wants to explore the marriage market, there is an entirely different set of rules to be followed. And different qualities to be sought.

So the dreary procession continued, each new failure confirming the unspoken understanding between the children that the only permanent people in their lives were themselves and their father.

Walter was in his late thirties when he first began to notice the quiet, attractive girl who worked in the little sub-post office in the village. Her name was Ruby Masters, and she lived in lodgings with old Mrs. Hardacre, who had nothing but praise for the retiring, well-spoken girl from 'up North somewhere'. According to the story, she had some weakness of the chest, and the doctors had suggested the softer airs of the South would benefit her. Both her parents were dead, she had a little money of her own, and so she had come to the unquestionable peace and quiet of Great Fording.

Ruby had been twenty three years old then, and such young men as were to be found in the area quickly joined the small queues for stamps at her counter. But whatever she was seeking in life did not appear to include rushing off to Winchester or Southampton, or one of the other size-able towns within reach. Walter took to posting his own letters, instead of asking one of the children to run down for him. Before anyone quite realised what was happening, Ruby Masters was married to a man fifteen years her senior, and set about making a good job of it.

To the children, she was at first merely the latest in a long line of housekeepers. But they soon found they had, not a new mother, but a new friend. A cheerful and happy companion, who transformed the whole atmosphere of the house, and their lives. Iris was fourteen by this time, and not a little puzzled as to why such a physically attractive young woman should tie herself down to someone like her father, who must be getting on for a hundred years old, and was quite a stick-in-the-mud. But there it was, and she quickly learned, not merely to accept the situation, but to love Ruby as she would have an older sister.

Matthew had no such problem. He quite simply adored

the pretty, sweet-smelling woman from the first day.

Now she was gone, torn from them cruelly, and they were back where they had been ten years ago, supporting each other, and their father.

They sat in comfortable silence for a time, then Matthew asked:

" What d'you think will happen, Icy?"

Iris knew perfectly well what he meant, but she wanted to delay answering as long as possible.

" Happen? What about?"

" About the cafe. About us, you and me. Well, about everything."

Iris hesitated.

" Could I have one of your cigarettes?"

" Sure."

Because she was only his sister, it didn't occur to Matt to extend the packet to her. Or produce a match. He simply jerked a thumb towards the bedside table, where the packet lay. Iris walked across, took one, and struck a match. In this dark part of the room, the sudden flare lit up her fine-chiselled features and the strong red mouth. Matt could never quite understand all the rave notices his sister received from all the boys in his year at school. And from a lot of the masters, too. They never said anything, naturally, but he couldn't fail to see the way they looked at her. Especially on the summer occasions, like Sports Day or the Annual Fete and Cricket Match. Iris was never short of people to rush around, finding ice-cream and cold drinks, no matter how long the queues were. Of course, they never saw her when she'd just washed her hair, or had a streaming cold. He said:

" Well? You haven't answered me."

She went back to the chair.

" I haven't answered you, because I don't know. Anyway, it's early days yet. Poor Ruby's funeral was only a week ago."

Iris watched with disapproval as he took another cigarette. It was too soon after the last one.

"You'll have to be going back soon, won't you? I mean, is there an exam this term?" asked Matt.

"No. Nothing. In any case the break is next week. It's not worth it. Sometime in January we start again. Sixteenth, eighteenth, I'm not sure exactly."

"Going to be a merry Christmas, isn't it? Wish we could go away, somewhere."

Iris sighed.

"Go away? Like where? In any case, Dad can't leave the café. You know that. When did he ever get away?"

Matt nodded.

"Funny sort of life, being tied like that. I mean, we're used to it, or we always have been, up to now. But it was—what do I mean, exactly—it was at second hand. Do you understand me? What I'm trying to say is, it was their place, Ruby's and Dad's. We only lived here, because we were the children. When we grew up, we would be like anybody else. Go away, get a job. Get married eventually, I suppose. But the café wasn't really ours. Not first-hand—oh Christ, I'm not getting this over at all."

"Yes, you are Matt. I know exactly what you mean."

Matt's stumbling explanation might not have made much sense to an outsider, but Iris understood him completely. Before Ruby's death, the position had been quite clear. She and Matthew would complete their studies, and then, with career objectives settled, they would each in turn go out into the world to make their way. Their father and Ruby were settled at the café, for as long as they wished to carry on. When they decided they had worked long enough, they could sell up, and lead a more ordinary kind of life. They could remain in Great Fording, or move away to the sea somewhere, do anything they liked. That was their life, a separate issue. She, Iris, would be off in some other direction, and Matt in yet another.

Ruby Ellis' murder had changed all that.

Walter Ellis couldn't run the place single-handed, even when he was fully recovered. Other people were helping out at the moment, but that was because of the circumstances. People always give a hand in times of disaster. But you couldn't expect them to go on forever. Before long, they would all have to be thinking in more permanent terms. And it was those permanent terms Iris didn't want to face up to. She was on the threshold of a good career. Once she completed her extra year, the following June, the world would be wide open. That was no more than the literal truth. She could go virtually anywhere, and be welcomed. The States, Africa, Far East, anywhere. Was she now being expected to give it all up? To offer herself in the place of Ruby? To spend every night of her life in that sweaty, fat-laden kitchen?

Or, if that wasn't exactly expected of her, was it her duty to offer? That was the real question, the one that kept her awake at night.

And Matt? What about him? He was bright, too. Not as clever as herself, academically, but a good sound worker, who could apply himself when he must. Was he to be denied his chance at a university place? Then there was the question of money. The café provided them all with a good, even high standard of living, but it was labour-intensive. It was one thing to have a member of the family working all night, weekends, Bank Holidays and so on, as a labour of love, or duty. To replace that member with a wage-earner, to expect those long unaided hours and conditions from an ordinary employee, was going to require an enormous wage-packet. Just imagine, she reflected, seven nights a week at twelve hours, including Saturdays and Sundays. Why, it must come to something like one hundred and fifty, or even perhaps two hundred pounds a week.

The family budget might be very healthy, but it couldn't stand that kind of outlay. So, what was the answer?

" Do you think it's my place to offer, Matt?"

" No."

The reply was immediate. Almost explosive. Iris waited for more.

" No bloody fear," he continued. " I've been thinking about this, Icy. There's you, and there's me. We've got our own lives to lead. I know it's hard on Dad, and all that, but it isn't our fault. If we were a couple of thicks, we might be very grateful for the café. But we're not. There's more in life for both of us than frying chips all night. I don't think the old man would want us to, anyway. He's always given us every chance. Can't see him changing now."

Iris leaned towards the partly opened window, and flicked ash outside.

" We might have to pull our weight for a while," she said tentatively.

Matthew swung his legs down from the bed, and sat upright, looking at her seriously.

" I've worked it all out, sister mine. It goes like this. I'm not due at university till October, next year. That means I'm free, for the moment."

" You've got this factory job—" she began.

Her brother held up a hand for silence.

" Never mind that. I get my turn later. You're first. Comes January, you get back to your course. I'll fry the chips. After you finish next summer, if you feel like frying chips for a month, I'll push off somewhere and have a holiday. After that, it's over. You start your career, I go to university. That's it."

Iris felt a flood of sudden relief, and hope.

" But the old man? What about him. I mean—"

" Look. At the moment, all we have here is disaster. Everything looks like collapsing around our ears. Nobody knows what's going to happen next week. Or even tomorrow, for that matter. With my plan, we all know exactly what we're doing for the best part of twelve months. That'll give Dad a good chance to sort himself out. Nobody can expect him to think straight at the moment. If we do it my way, he doesn't have to. Everybody knows where they stand, and Dad has a year's grace. It's the only way, Icy."

His sister rose, and went slowly across to where he was sitting. Then she sat beside him, put her arms around his neck, and kissed him gently on the cheek.

" Bless you, Matt. I don't know what else to say. It's a wonderful way out. Quite perfect. I've been racking my brains with worry."

He grinned, and patted her awkwardly on the back.

" That's all right, little sister. Big brother Matt will take care of all your problems."

She tousled his hair.

" Big brother is right. I should have talked to you before. Only—"

" Only what?"

" Well—don't get cross now—I've been thinking that everything falls on my shoulders. You know, the way it used to."

He looked into her eyes. Poor old Icy. He'd almost forgotten how much he had relied on her at every turn, all those years ago. Now he winked solemnly.

" Old enough to die for my country, let me remind you. That's old enough to fry a few chips."

She wanted to say more, much more, but knew that they had reached the stage where further talk would be superfluous. And embarrassing. Instead she winked back, and stood up.

" That's what we'll call you," she decided. " Chip-sergeant

Ellis."

" I don't think the work justifies the rank," he countered. " Chip-corporal would be high enough to start with."

" Fair enough." She went and looked out of the window.

The café was busy again today. The ranks of various-sized lorries were drawn in neat lines across the forecourt. For a day or two there had been a big drop in business, because of the police activity around the place. But things seemed to be back to normal again.

" Icy?"

" H'm?"

" Do you know something?"

" What?"

Iris half turned her head.

" This is the longest time we've been alone together without talking about the murder."

She walked over to the bedside table, and took another cigarette.

" Hey—"

" I'll pay you back. I've got some downstairs."

" Well?" he pressed.

" Well what?" she hedged. " There's nothing to talk about, is there? We've talked until we're blue in the face. The plain fact is, neither of us can come up with anything new. We're just as much in the dark as the police are."

" I know. It's just that I keep thinking there must be some little thing we've been overlooking. Something that will throw a new light on the whole thing."

" Only on the films, Matt. In real life the police don't miss a thing."

" Well, I hope so. Hope they catch the bastard."

There was sudden anger in his voice, and the girl at the window looked around with sympathy.

" Don't worry about that. They'll catch him. It may not be this week, or next, but they'll have him."

" I hope you're right." But he said it without conviction.

She had a sudden impulse to tell him, but checked herself in time. No. Definitely no. It would be a wrong thing to do. She'd kept it to herself all this time. She would carry on. In any case, it would be nothing but selfishness, on her part. A desire to share the problem with someone. Pure selfishness. There was nothing whatever to be gained, outside of her own relief, and it certainly wouldn't help Matt. There was a great deal of difference between being old enough to be a chip-corporal, and old enough to share her particular burden. Bless his heart, he was so proud of himself for coming up with his plan. It would scarcely be an act of generosity on her part to involve him with this thing.

" Icy?"

" H'm?"

" When they catch this chap, you don't suppose they'd let me have five minutes alone with him, do you? Sort of ask him a few questions?"

She shook her head.

" No way. Dad already asked them that. I was there when he did it. They were quite understanding about it, but the answer was definitely no."

" Pity."

A blue Austin-Maxi turned in off the main road, drove around the side of the café, and pulled up in front of the house.

" Talk of the devils," announced Iris. " They're back again."

" Wonder what they want?"

Matt got up from the bed, and joined her looking down outside.

" That's Mr. Barnett, the inspector," he recognised. " I know the other one, too. What's his name? Only been here once, the day after it happened. He's the inspector's boss."

"Superintendent Morgan, if I remember right."

"That's right. Perhaps they've got some news. You coming down?"

Matt was already at the door.

"You bet I am. It'll have to be pretty good news to justify getting Dad out of bed."

They went rapidly down the stairs, making as little noise as possible. The front door bell had only given one ping when Matt opened the door, and they saw the grave faces of the police officers.

"Good morning," said Barnett, keeping his voice flat. "Is your father at home?"

"Yes—"

They both spoke together, but Matt stopped, to let Iris answer.

"Yes, he is, Mr. Barnett, but he's asleep. It's the first decent sleep he's had since—since the murder. So, if you could come back please, or if I could get him to drive into town this afternoon—?"

But the other one, the superintendent, was already shouldering his way inside the house.

"I'm afraid that won't do, Miss Ellis. Let us in, please."

Although he was polite enough, there was to be no gainsaying his entrance. His whole attitude made that clear.

"In the bedroom, is he?"

Iris nodded, beginning to feel alarmed.

"Yes, I'll go and—"

"No need to bother you, Miss. We'll just go straight up."

But Matt stood between them and the stairs.

"Just hold on," he said aggressively. "Have you got a warrant to come barging in here?"

Superintendent Morgan was about to retort, then changed

his mind and swallowed. When he spoke, his voice was almost kindly.

"Yes son, I'm afraid we have. Now, be a good chap, don't go making things difficult for us."

Matt wavered, and looked uncertainly at the one he knew, Inspector Barnett.

Barnett nodded.

"Let us by, Matt."

He stood against the wall, worried now, and looking to Iris for comfort. But there was none on her face. She was just as bothered as he was, as they watched the two officers climb the stairs.

They did not bother to knock at the bedroom door, but opened it quickly and stepped inside.

Matthew and Iris tiptoed up the stairs to the open door. Morgan's voice was loud and commanding.

"Walter Brian Ellis, I have here a warrant for your arrest on the charge that you did murder Ruby Jane Ellis—"

Matthew caught Iris, in time to prevent her from falling downstairs.

FOUR

The early afternoon sun was quite strong for December, making the office stuffy. Jack Bradford opened a window, and leaned there for a moment, watching the busy crowds hurrying up one side of Villiers Street, and down the other. They never ceased to amaze him, always so determined to get to wherever it was, or home from wherever it had been. At this time of year it was at its peak, because of the heavy injection of Christmas shoppers. These were easily identi-fied by the two feet square advertisements they all carried, in the shape of carrier-bags with the names of West End stores clearly displayed.

The unexpected warm weather had tempted some of the girls to shed their greys and dark blues, and retrieve some of the brighter colours from the normal winter hiber-nation. Bradford stayed there for a few minutes, enjoying the girls. It was his contention that a man with a window in Villiers Street didn't need to watch television. The pasty-faced dollies on the box were no match for the genuine articles which paraded daily for his pleasure, on their way down to the Embankment tube station. He looked at his watch. It was two thirty-seven and nine seconds, he learned. Better stick around till about half past three, for the sake of appearances. Besides, there was nothing to do until seven that evening. That's what he missed about hav-ing left the force. You could never say you were bored, in those days. In fact, quite the reverse. There were never enough hours in the day, you never felt you finished any-thing properly, and there was always twice as much work waiting to be done as there had been the last time you looked. Boredom was unheard of. Not that he'd go back now, mind you. There had been a time, in the early days, when he'd spend hours, scheming and plotting how to get his old job back. He'd bribe a few doctors, falsify medical reports, x-rays and so on. But it had all been a dream, and it would never have worked. Anyway, the phase had long passed. He didn't want to go back now.

John Andrew Bradford had wanted to be a policeman ever since he was twelve years old. There had been an armed robbery at the off-licence in the little shopping precinct near his home. The group of small boys on bicycles stopped their fooling around, and stared aghast at the wild-eyed figure which burst suddenly from the off-licence, brandishing a revolver. It all seemed like something on the telly. The young police officer seemed to materialise from nowhere and advance towards the thief. The boys watched in terrified fascination, waiting for the bandit to shoot down the unarmed policeman. But the officer continued to walk steadily forward, calling on the man to give himself up. Instead of shooting him, the thief turned suddenly away, to start running. The police officer ran two or three paces, then launched himself at the retreating man, in a tremendous flying tackle. The gun hit the pavement and went off.

But no one was hurt, except for the prostrate villain. Young Jack expected to read all about the affair on the front page of his father's newspaper the next day, but he was to be disappointed. He finally found an item, buried half way down page six, but it did not do justice to the real-life drama he had personally witnessed. In his mind, that young policeman should have been awarded the Victoria Cross at least, and a pension for life.

His own course was settled from that day onwards. He was going to be a policeman, and nothing would shake him from it. People did try to divert him, parents and schoolmasters alike. Because Jack was bright, and ought to go to university, and become something in one of the professions. So far as he was concerned, the profession of policeman was what he wanted.

Luckily, the police agreed with him. He was tall, six feet one inch, a good weight for height ratio, useful at team games, and quick with his paperwork. He made a good copper, as all his superiors agreed, and at twenty eight was one of the youngest Detective Inspectors at the Yard, when the blow came.

There'd been a fracas with a warehouse gang, and Jack Bradford had been one of three officers injured in the melee. While he was in the hospital, every possible check had been

41

run on him, to ensure that no internal injuries were over-looked. After his discharge, following four days of blissful rest, punctuated by endless chatting up of the nurses, Bradford reported back for duty.

"Inspector, I've got a bit of disturbing news, here."

The chief super didn't seem to want to look him straight in the eye.

"News, sir?"

"The people in the hospital think they've detected a heart murmur."

A heart murmur. He didn't even know what it implied.

"Sir?"

"It means you may have a dicky heart. Sorry to put it to you so bluntly, but there's no hiding the facts. I'm not going to accept it, of course. We'll have you run over properly. Finest doctors in London, you needn't worry about that. But meantime, I'm afraid you'll have to be on sick leave."

"Sick leave? Me? But I'm all right guvnor. Fit as a fiddle."

His departmental head sighed.

"I'm sure you feel well, and I sincerely hope you are. For your own sake, as well as ours."

Bradford didn't like the sound of those last words at all.

"What does that mean sir, as well as yours?"

"It means, inspector, that if these findings are con-firmed, you're going to have to be released."

"Released," he echoed. "Do you mean I'll get the sack?"

"No, of course I don't. Not the sack. We don't sack people like you, Jack. But it could mean you'll have to go. Anyway, don't let's look on the black side. You go off on leave, and we'll see what happens. Might be noth-ing to it."

But he'd known there was, even from that first interview. And one month later, to the day, he found he was ex-Detective Inspector Bradford. After the initial period of shocked disbelief, and wild scheming as to how to get himself restored, he moved into a second stage of self-pity, accompanied by a lot of heavy drinking. Then, one day, he woke up with a solution in his head. They wouldn't let him be a copper, not one of their coppers. Very well, he'd set up his own police force. On his force, they wouldn't fire people with dicky hearts, because the boss would see to that. And so, he became John A. Bradford, Confidential Enquiries. There would be no money in it, of course. Thirty pounds a day, plus expenses, and probably an average of three days work per week, if he was lucky. But that wouldn't be the whole story. Because John A. Bradford would have another source of income, and he knew exactly where to find it.

All over London, small shopkeepers paid out various sums of money every week to so-called protection agencies, in order to ensure that their premises were not wrecked, stocks ruined and so forth. If they refused to pay, then the destruction would inevitably follow, and the destroyers would bear a remarkable resemblance to the representatives of the protection agency. Some of the braver, or more foolish, might take proceedings, but the cases never reached a courtroom. Even if the odd one slipped through, the accusing shopkeeper suddenly found he could not identify those responsible. It was all very neat, all very sad, and there was nothing the police could do.

That was where Jack Bradford came in. He knew the racket, through and through. Knew the victims, and villains alike. He introduced an agency of his own, but one with a difference. One with no reprisals. Where the small traders had been paying sums ranging from twenty to fifty pounds every week, he would charge ten. Five of these would produce an official printed receipt, for the benefit of the Inland Revenue, and five would go into his pocket, for the benefit of John A. Bradford.

The shopkeepers liked the idea, and they liked to be dealing with a man with all Bradford's police connections. But they were reluctant to change, because of the reprisals from the existing people. Bradford had selected his area with care. It wasn't too large, because he knew there would be a confrontation with the thugs whose territory it was. He didn't want to have to fight one of the big London gangs, not because he was afraid, but because he couldn't win. The team he would be up against consisted of only four hard-line villains. He persuaded a couple of the hardier shopkeepers to give him a chance. They did so, and the thugs reacted swiftly. Windows were smashed, petrol scattered over valuable stocks. But Bradford was ready for them. So were the five newly-retired police officers whom he had recruited solely for the purpose on a short-term basis. There was a bloody set-to, which ended with three of the thugs and two of his assistants in the hospital. Prosecutions were brought by the Small Traders Mutual Trust, President John A. Bradford, and the villains were put away. After that, the rest of the shopowners came clamouring for membership, and Bradford found himself comfortably placed overnight. There were thirty sets of premises involved. At ten pounds a week apiece, that meant three hundred a week, by way of income. One-fifty was official, one-fifty tax-free. Bradford was a happy man.

Happy, but neither too greedy, nor foolish. People came to call on him, smooth-faced lawyers, with brief cases. Mr. Bradford's success had been noted with pleasure by several sources. There was, however, concern in certain business quarters, about the extent to which he, Mr. Bradford, intended to develop his interests. These could conflict with the interests of others, who would find the situation unacceptable. He, Mr. Bradford, told them not to worry. He was quite satisfied with things as they were, and was not an over-ambitious man. Naturally, he would be most vigorous in pursuing the best interests of his own organisation, but he would not be interfering with others.

The smooth-faced men had gone away, and there had been no further trouble. And so, all Jack Bradford had to do was to stroll around his little domain every day, shake hands with all the proprietors, and keep his ear to the ground, for news of any set of villains who might seek to move in.

The air in the office was sweeter now, and sun or no sun, it was turning chilly. Reluctantly, he watched one last girl, a tall, free-striding brunette, swinging a leather shoulder bag and flashing her sparkling teeth at some lucky young man who strode beside her possessively. All right for some, reflected the watching man sourly. Why wasn't he at work, that chap?

He closed the window, and went back to his leather-topped desk, which was bare except for two newspapers, each open at the racing forecasts for the day. He looked at his watch again. The two forty-five at Chepstow would just have begun.

There was a knock at the door. He looked up, without much interest. A girl came in. She was about five feet six, one hundred and twenty pounds, with shining fair hair and a smiling, confident face. A knockout, he decided. Maybe some kind soul had sent her to him for Christmas. They inspected each other for a few seconds.

Bradford was on his feet by now, and half-smiling at the newcomer.

" Mr. Bradford?"

Nice voice, too. Sort of musical.

" Yes. Please come in, won't you?"

She closed the door, and walked up to the desk. He in-

dicated a chair and sat himself down. When she was
settled, she said:

" I'm Miss Ellis. Iris Ellis. I'm hoping you can help
me."

Iris Ellis. That wasn't as musical as the voice. Still, Iris
was nice.

" I hope so too, Miss Ellis. Suppose you tell me the
problem."

" Do you mind if I smoke?"

" Please. Here, take one of these."

He kept a large silver box of cigarettes on the desk. It
impressed the visitors, he'd found, and for some reason to
convey an impression of solidity. A smoke out of a packet
is just a fag, someone had once told him, but a smoke from
a silver box is a cigarette.

" Thank you."

He clicked the big ivory lighter, and held it for her. She
was playing for time, of course. Most people did. Silly,
really, because it would have to come out in the end. He
hoped she wouldn't turn out to be one of those girls who
wanted the name of an abortion doctor. That would have
been a disappointment, with this one.

She began talking, rather nervously.

" I've been to a lot of trouble to find you, Mr. Bradford."

" Oh? Well, I don't advertise much, it's true. But I'm
in the Yellow Pages."

Funny, the way the dying sun caught her hair. Made it
almost reddish. Very attractive.

" Yes, I know. I've been working my way through them.
I suppose I'm lucky your name begins with a ' B '."

There was not much he could say to that, so he just
looked pleasant, and waited.

" I've been to them all, you see."

" Oh. And couldn't they meet your needs?"

Bad start. Plenty of good people before him, alphabetically. This must be crooked as hell, whatever it was. She wagged her head, and the sun danced.

" I didn't approach them. Didn't go inside." Then she tumbled ahead, the explanatory words spilling out rapidly. " I needed a one-man concern, for one thing. And I wanted a younger man. Most of them seem to be in their fifties. And I wanted a man whose face I thought I could trust."

She stopped as quickly as she had begun, and looked at him.

" Let me understand you, Miss Ellis. Do you mean you've had us all under some kind of surveillance "—a nod to that —" and kept on looking at us, in turn, before you actually approached someone?"

" Yes," she replied, seriously. " I've been here since before lunch. I saw you go out, and I was here again when you came back. I decided to come in."

" You couldn't have been loitering outside," he objected. " No disrespect, Miss Ellis, but I wouldn't have missed a girl who looks like you."

She wasn't at all put out, and the half-smile was almost mischievous.

" No. I was sitting in the window of the sandwich-bar opposite."

" Ah." But he still had one more objection. " It's half an hour since I came back from lunch. You took your time."

" Yes. Even after I thought my mind was made up, there was still the question of getting my courage together. But I'm here now."

" And I'm very pleased you are. So, could we talk about it now?"

She tapped her cigarette nervously against the wide glass ashtray.

" Before I tell you the problem, let me tell you about

my hesitation. I don't know the law, you see."

" About this reservation," he prompted.

" Well, this thing I want to talk about, it could be, and I only say ' could be ', I'm not certain, but it could be connected with something the police are already working on. Does that mean, in your position, that you would have to go to the police with it? I mean, would you have a legal obligation?"

Ah. Bradford considered his reply, then shook his head.

" No, not necessarily. Let me put it this way. I most certainly would under no circumstances conceal anything criminal. The very best I could do on that, would be to show you the door. I couldn't take it on myself to hide evidence, either. There are many factors involved, Miss Ellis. It could be that you're worrying unnecessarily. You're going to have to tell me something, or we'll never get any-where. To start with, leaving out the details, what crime is it the police have under investigation?"

Iris took a deep breath, leaned forward, and stared levelly into his eyes.

" The crime is murder."

The room seemed suddenly cold.

" I think you'd better tell me more."

FIVE

Iris told him.

Bradford remembered the case at once, but not in detail. At first, it had sounded, from the newspaper reports, like a fairly ordinary case of an intruder who'd lost his nerve,

48

and committed murder for a few hundred pounds. Small-time stuff, uninteresting. Then, when the husband had been charged, it became very ordinary indeed. A sordid little case all round, almost boring in its routine nature. Nothing in to excite the interest, even of a policeman, unless he was one of those actually assigned to the case.

But of course, to those involved it was the greatest tragedy that had ever happened. The girl was good with description, good with her absorption in detail. Make a good witness, this one. He listened with great care, his mind alert for omissions, vital pieces left out. Because, if there was anything in her visit which had a bearing on the case against Walter Ellis, then Bradford was quite clear as to where his duty lay. And it did not lie in helping this girl obstruct the course of justice, pretty as she was.

"And that's the whole story is it, Miss Ellis? You haven't left anything out?"

"No."

The girl dropped her eyes at the moment she uttered the denial. There was more to come. Bradford was prepared to wait for it.

"No, there's nothing else about the murder," she said quietly.

The private detective spread his hands.

"Well, then?"

"It's something else. Something that happened afterwards. I had to clear out her clothes, you see. It's a woman's job, and I'm the only one. At the back of her wardrobe was the usual pile of old shoes. Some women can't throw them away. You probably know that."

He tried to look like a man who knew all about women's old shoes.

"There was one pair of knee-length boots. Must have been quite expensive when they were new. I can't recall ever having seen Ruby wear them. In one of them was a

rolled envelope. I opened it, not knowing what to expect."
Iris unfastened the clip on her sling bag, and brought
out an A4 size envelope, rolled into a tube, and secured by
a rubber band. "This is it. You'd better see for yourself."

He took the rolled package from her, sliding off the
rubber band. The envelope immediately sprang almost to
a flat position. So there was something more inside than
ordinary paper. The end had been slit open. He looked at
Iris as she watched with rapt attention. Sliding two fingers
inside, he felt something shiny, and pulled it out.

There were three photographs, all studio sizes, all professional work. They were publicity shots, or he was very
much mistaken. All three were of the same girl, a dark-
haired beauty in her early twenties. In the first she wore
a top hat and a bow tie. Nothing else, except for small
white collars at the tip of each of the splendid breasts.
The picture was half length. The second pose had her
leaning back on a chaise-longue, the dark hair falling down
behind her neck. She wore a see-through negligee in this
one, which fell away to reveal the whole length of long,
straight legs. Bradford placed the two side by side, and
turned to the last portrait. This had been taken from a
downward angle, so that the girl was looking up at the
viewer, her full mouth open to reveal the sparkling even
teeth. Slim manicured hands cupped her naked breasts
upwards in invitation.

Bradford caught his breath. These weren't the first girlie
pictures he'd ever seen, but the quality of the work, and of
the girl, were unusual. He placed the three pictures in a row
and took another long look. The same photographer had
taken all three, and the inscription 'Tony Jervis—London'
appeared in the right-hand corner. If the girl had said she
found the photographs in her father's desk, he could have
understood that. But what would some countrywoman want,
with stuff like this? It made no sense.

" Have you any idea why your stepmother should have pictures of this kind? I mean, did she perhaps know the girl, or something?"

Iris nodded strangely.

" Oh yes. She knew her all right. The girl in those pictures is my stepmother."

Bradford didn't exactly let his jaw drop open, but the effect was the same.

" This—this is—was—"

" Yes. You're no more surprised than I was, Mr. Bradford. There are several family photographs of Ruby around the house, and you may rest assured that none of them look like that."

" M'm."

He didn't quite believe it, yet. Not after the word-picture he'd had of Ruby Ellis, and the family life the girl had described.

" It couldn't possibly be a sister, perhaps—"

" There is no sister," she interrupted. " That's why I'm here Mr. Bradford. Ruby had been married to my father for eight years. There's no chance of her having led a double life in that time. If you knew Great Fording, you would know what I mean. Prior to that, she was in digs in the village for quite some time—"

"—how long?" he cut in.

" I'm not sure exactly. A year, perhaps, give or take a few months. And there was nothing questionable about her conduct during that time either. A village watches everybody, and a pretty girl gets watched twice as hard as anybody else."

" Yes, I know that's true. Let's see, you said your stepmother was thirty two when she died?"

" Thirty three."

" Sorry. Thirty three, then. Married eight years, living in the village a year before that, give or take a little. So

51

she would have been twenty three or four when she first appeared."

Iris nodded her agreement, and pointed to the photographs.

"Exactly. And how old is that girl? My age, a year or two either way. Oh, I'm twenty two, by the way. She would have been roughly my age, when those pictures were taken."

"Yes, I see."

Bradford was beginning to be intrigued, despite himself. A girl would have to be really fed up with life, to leave the bright lights and bury herself so completely—and successfully—in the sticks. Very fed up. Or very frightened. He looked down at the three faces in front of him. This girl would not have been easy to frighten, he decided.

"Did Ruby ever talk to you about her past?"

"Not about anything like that," denied Iris. "We always understood she'd had a couple of unimportant office jobs, up in Liverpool, before she decided to come south. London was never mentioned, I'm certain. But that's where those were taken."

"Yes, I saw that. Liverpool, you say. Did she speak with any accent at all?"

"If you mean did she sound like some of those comedians on the television, the answer is no. But there was a slight touch of the north in the way she spoke. It was soft, not aggressive. Very pleasant to hear."

"So you think it would be safe to believe she really did come from somewhere in the north at some time?"

Iris was very positive about that.

"No doubt at all. It used to make us laugh, the way she'd get cross if someone local couldn't distinguish between Lancashire and Yorkshire. You know, we tend to get a bit mixed up down here, sometimes. Ruby would be very quick to set us right."

Bradford nodded. The girl's head was very close across the desk, as they both stared at the photographs. She smelt delicious. Abruptly, he pulled himself back, turned sideways, and rested an uncompromising arm lengthwise on the leather surface.

" I know what you mean, Miss Ellis. Let me bring you back to the present. You went through your step-mother's wardrobe, found these," he tapped his fingers, " and they puzzled you. That's natural. They'd have puzzled me too, in the circumstances. But why bring them to me?"

Iris wrinkled her brow.

" I should have thought that was obvious. I want to know more about them. I want someone to look into the situation."

" Miss Ellis, forgive me, but what bearing can all this possibly have on the lady's murder? I don't want to be brutal, and I appreciate what you must be suffering on account of your father, but how are these old glamour shots going to help him?"

Iris shrugged, frowning slightly.

" I don't know," she admitted. " You probably think I'm clutching at straws. Well, perhaps I am, but at least I'm trying to do something positive. If I could find out what these mean—"

"—you would know what your step-mother was doing ten years ago," he finished. " How far forward does that get you? Look, Miss Ellis, I'm a stranger, and I've no axe to grind. Let me tell you how I see the situation, before you go any further with this."

He waited, to ensure that she was paying proper attention. There was something in the set of her chin that warned him he was wasting his time, but he went ahead.

" Your step-mother has been murdered, your father has been charged with that crime. You are looking for something, anything, that may help to clear your father. I would

53

do the same thing. You find these pictures, which are ten years old, and you don't understand them. Because they are strange to you, because they don't fit your understanding of your step-mother, you want them explained. It's a very short step, from there, to thinking they may be of help to your father. Believe me, you're barking up a gum tree. Ten years might as well be a lifetime. If you're hoping I'll find some mysterious lover from those days, who has been yearning for Ruby Ellis all this time, suddenly released, and murdered her, then you are deceiving yourself, and I'm not going to help you do it. If that sounds brutal, then I'm sorry. But it's better than taking your money under false pretences. Take my word for it, you are wasting your time."

She listened, with her head set slightly to one side.

"Do you always turn your prospective clients away like that?"

"If I don't think I can help them, yes. If I take on an investigation and fail, that's one thing. I know I'll have tried. But to take on a thing like this, based on false hopes, that's a different matter altogether. I don't see anything here that could help your father, and any investigator will tell you the same, if he's honest."

Iris nodded seriously.

"Thank you. What you have been saying, these last few minutes, has helped to clear my own mind. You're quite right, about my hopes for my father, but that isn't the whole of it. There's Ruby, as well. I loved that woman, almost as if she were my own mother. I have my own memories of her, built up over the years. I can't reconcile those memories with these—these things. It's almost as though my own life has been an unreality, a false existence. I know that if I don't find out the truth, then in time I shall supply my own explanation. In time, I shall come to hate her. That isn't a very nice prospect, Mr. Bradford, and it's

54

damned unfair to Ruby, after all she's done for me. I owe it to her to prevent that happening if I can. So, I understand what you've said, and I appreciate your consideration. But I would still like you to look into this for me. Will you do it?"

Jack Bradford didn't want the job. He didn't need the work, or the money. What he wanted was to go home, and check through the racing results. He looked into the pretty, troubled face.

"Very well," he sighed. "But not for long. This is a big city, Miss Ellis. It eats up girls, the way a child eats up cornflakes. This is London, not Great Fording. Last year's girls are no more than a memory. A girl from ten years back—"

He shrugged.

"But you will try?"

"I'll try it for a few days. No more."

She held out her hand impulsively. He took it, smiling slightly.

"It'll cost you thirty pounds a day. Plus expenses."

"I thought it would be more," she replied.

You'll find it's enough, after a few days, he thought. They always do. Aloud, he said:

"Did you happen to bring her birth certificate with you?"

"Why—er—no. I didn't think of it."

"But there is one, at home?"

"There must be, I imagine. Shall I look for it?"

"Please. Give me a ring when you find it. The number's on here."

He handed over one of his small business cards. She put it carefully away. Bradford hoped she'd be able to locate it, among all the junk which he could see inside her bag.

"I'll just need a note of your own address and telephone number."

55

He drew a pad of paper towards him, and scribbled down her instructions.

" Thank you, Miss Ellis. Don't forget that birth certificate."

" I won't. And thank you."

For a moment, he thought she was going to kiss him, in her relief. She might get a surprise, if she did. But the moment was gone. So, too, was the girl.

Bradford ambled across to the window, thinking. On the street outside, the homegoers were thickening now, hurrying down to the tube, as though their lives depended on it. As though they had to escape from the great jaws of the metropolis before curfew.

The way she must have done once, the girl whose pictures lay on his desk.

That could have been her, there, the one in the camel-hair coat. Or that one, in the grey leather two-piece. Or that one—

He turned away, shaking his head.

It was hopeless.

SIX

That same evening, Inspector Joe Barnett yawned, stretched, and looked at his watch. It was twenty past seven, and he had been on duty for more than twelve hours, except for fifteen minutes in the local pub, for a half pint of keg bitter and a flabby sandwich. One day, he promised himself, he was going to get a job where he would get home before his children went to bed. There were people in the world, if gossip was to be believed, who not only saw their children every day, but actually had an hour to play with them, find out how they were progressing. Mind you, little Bobbie didn't go upstairs until seven thirty. If he went now—no. If he went now, that daunting heap of blue and grey forms would still be there to greet him, first thing in the morning, and no copper in his right mind wanted that. In this job, there was one vital lesson to be learned, and the earlier in his career a man learned it, the longer he could stave off a nervous breakdown. Never let the paper get ahead of you. That was the lesson. Never mind the villains, the hours, the rougher aspects of the work. The real enemy was the paper. Once a man let that get an edge on him, he was due for a hard life.

Barnett sighed, took a sip from his mug of half-cold tea, and picked up his pen again. There were voices in the corridor outside, but he ignored them, grinding away at an Information Received sheet.

A man stuck his head round the door.

" Evening, inspector. You got a minute?"

He looked up, unsmiling.

" Why not? I've only been here twelve hours. Seems a pity not to stay the full twenty four, now."

But he spoke without rancour. Sergeant Tom Hammond was a fellow-sufferer, but he did his suffering on the other shift. The newcomer entered, opened a packet of cigarettes, and held them out to the seated man.

" Thanks." Barnett took one. " Just come on?"

" Yes. Should have gone straight to bed, really. Been in London all day. Christmas shopping. Those pavements must be the hardest in the world. If they play up a copper's feet, what must they do to ordinary people?"

" I know what you mean. Especially shopping. I hate that job. I think they must have special hard pavements for it. Get anything good?"

Hammond shrugged.

57

" Got what I could afford. The prices this year are worse than ever."

" Don't let my wife hear you. It's her favourite subject."

Barnett waited. Hammond wouldn't have come in just to pass the time of day. The sergeant leaned his hands on the desk.

" Saw a friend of yours."

" Ah."

" Thought you'd be interested. Iris Ellis."

Of course, Walter's daughter. Barnett had met a lot of new people since the Ellis investigation, and in any case he'd only seen the daughter twice. But a man doesn't forget an attractive woman like that overnight.

" Really? Lovely girl, that. In London, you say? What's the date?" He looked at the calendar. " Thought so. She ought to be at the university. They don't finish their term for a few days yet. Probably too much to do around the café. Did you speak to her?"

" No. She probably wouldn't remember me, anyway."

" You remembered her, though. Dirty old man. What was she up to?"

The sergeant's face was serious.

" Well, that's why I came in. I was on my way to the tube, to come home. The girl suddenly walked out of a café, a few yards in front of me. She walked straight across the street, and disappeared into a doorway. I thought it was odd."

" Odd? Why? People go in doorways all the time?"

" Yes, but not down there. Not exactly residential, is it?"

Barnett sighed.

" Look Tom, you'll have to go a bit slower. What do you mean, not down there? Down where? I don't even know what part of London we're in."

Hammond nodded quickly.

58

" Sorry. My fault. When I said the tube, I meant the Embankment station. I was walking down Villiers Street. That's the street that runs down from Charing Cross station to the river. It's all cafés, or nearly. Are you with me now?"

Barnett's face cleared.

" Ah yes. I'm with you. They have a band playing down the bottom in the summer."

" You've got it. So, as I say, I was curious about who she was going to see. It's only a narrow street, so it was no trouble to cross over. This doorway was between the shops, and the upper floors are quite often used for small offices. The one she went to had a plate outside. Seemed to be a one-room business, two at the most."

" And what was it called?"

" It was called," and Hammond paused for the announcement, " The Small Traders Mutual Trust."

Barnett made a face.

" Never heard of it."

" Nor me. But I got to thinking. When you were working on that Ellis murder with the super, we all got roped in for donkey work, at different times. There was one side of the case, never came to anything. I was involved a couple of times. We were trying to establish whether there was any chance of the racket in goods-lost-in-transit being connected with your enquiries. As it happened, there seemed to be no connection, and it fizzled out."

If Barnett hadn't been so tired, he would have cottoned on more quickly.

" Yes, I remember. So, what about it?"

Hammond looked injured.

" What about it?" he repeated. " Well, perhaps nothing, but I thought you ought to know. Here's a girl, from a café on a major trunk road, a transport café, no less, paying a visit to some twopenny ha'penny outfit with a name like that, in an area like that. And right next door to one of London's big stations. I just thought it was worth passing on. Well, it's your case, of course."

Barnett held up a hand.

"Now, don't go getting sniffy, Tom. I'm just a bit slow on the thinking at the moment. Yes, I do see what you mean. Certainly, it'll be worth asking a couple of questions. Could be a very nice bonus, if there's anything in it. More for the Regional people, really. Still, we're all coppers, eh?"

"Right. On top of that, it'd be one up for the country boys, if we can turn up something they couldn't find, eh?"

They both grinned.

"Let me write that name down, Tom."

Hammond repeated the name.

"Bloke who runs it is called Bradford. John A. Bradford."

Barnett grunted, as he wrote.

"C.R.O. might know him. No harm in asking. Thanks Tom. I'll let you know what happens. And Tom—"

"Don't worry, I won't."

"Won't what?"

"You were going to say, don't mention it to anybody else at the moment. I'm not going to."

"Good. Might be nothing in it. No need to make ourselves look silly."

"Agreed. Well, I'd better get on. Hope I don't get a surveillance tonight. Don't think my feet'll stand it."

"Thanks again. Tom. Goodnight."

When he'd gone, Barnett looked around the room. Where was that business directory?

*   *   *

The sky was dark and overcast when Iris emerged from the station. It was the end of her second consecutive day in London, looking for a suitable enquiry agency, and she

60

was feeling tired. Tired, but not dispirited, because it seemed to her that Mr. Bradford was a real find. Many of the other people she'd inspected, from a safe distance, were also former police officers, but none of them retained any of the zest and almost youthfulness of her final choice. Not that he was a youth, by any means. Probably in his early thirties, but despite his necessary formality there was a spring in his movements, to which she had responded thankfully. What was it old Miss Meadows used to say? Youth is not a matter of birthdays, my girl, but an attitude to the world. She grinned. Miss Meadows had a dozen cliches which could be applied to every human situation. Rather like betting on every horse in the race, she'd always felt. And, on that subject, Mr. Bradford seemed to take quite an interest in horse-racing. Perhaps he'd be interested in coming to look round Major Frederick's stables one day? You're going too fast again, my girl. You'd do better to be looking for a taxi.

A shadow crossed her face, at her own reminder. A taxi out to Great Fording was going to cost her two pounds, and it was too far to walk. In the past, the cost would never have entered her reckoning. But those days were gone. Ever since her father's arrest, she had become more and more conscious of how much everything cost. There was going to have to be a reckoning. Not immediately, not for some months, perhaps. But inevitably. It was so very hard to attempt to get to grips with long-term problems of that kind. She wouldn't be able to take account of—no. She certainly couldn't count on that. There was only one thing in life that mattered, and that was her father's trial. That had to be dealt with, first. Once he was home again, they would all have to have a serious conference. Her father, Matt and herself.

But suppose he wasn't acquitted? Supposing—

A car horn parped nearby.

" Iris? That is Iris, isn't it?"

In the murky yellow light from the station she couldn't quite make out the driver's face.

" Mr. Parsons?"

" The very same. Are you going home? Hop in, if you are."

" Thank you very much."

She walked around to the other side of the car, with mixed feelings. Since Ruby's murder, and more particularly since her father's arrest, she had kept her contact with the village people to a minimum. Not that they had been anything but nice to her, but she felt awkward. And particularly with Mr. Parsons, who owned the general store and sub post-office. The very one in which Ruby had worked, all those years ago.

" There's a safety harness there, if you don't mind, Iris. Don't like 'em myself, but you never know."

She buckled the thick strap around herself, as he started the engine. For no good reason she found herself thinking back to earlier years, when Matt and she would play Happy Families. It always seemed wrong to them that Mr. Parsons should be a shopkeeper. Mr. Parsons ought to be the vicar. The vicar, in those days, was a man named Mead. Clearly, the vicar should be the landlord of an inn.

" You're looking a bit tired, Iris."

" Am I? I've just been up to London. It's a tiring place."

" You're right there. And you've got a lot on your mind, of course."

She wished he'd talk about the weather, or something. Anything. But Adam Parsons chose otherwise.

" Iris, I've known you since you were born, so let me say something. It may sound all too easy, coming from an outsider, but I'm going to say it, just the same. Try not to worry too much. This is all a dreadful mistake, but it won't last forever."

She turned to look at his so-familiar profile, with the grey moustache drooping at the side of his mouth.

"Mistake?"

He nodded emphatically.

"Sheer nonsense, the whole thing. Believe me, I know. I don't care what those idiots think. I've known Walter Ellis since we were boys. Before you were ever thought of. He could never have done it."

Iris felt a strong impulse to put her arms around this fat, middle-aged man, funny moustache included.

"You don't think my father could do it? Commit—murder, I mean?"

"Didn't say that. We all could, I suppose. Catch us on the wrong day, and we all could, Lord help us. But not like that, not Walter. He might hit somebody, if they drove him hard enough. Bash 'em with a hammer, or something. But he couldn't have done that. And, most especially, not to Ruby. No possibility of it. They'll find out, you'll see."

Unable to prevent herself, Iris began to weep. Mr. Parsons nodded.

"You carry on. It'll make you feel better. There are some Kleenex in the glove-box."

After that, they drove in silence, Iris mopping at her eyes, and telling herself not to be such a fool. Finally, they arrived at her house. She climbed out thankfully, not speaking. Then, she suddenly leaned back into the car, and kissed the astonished driver hard on the cheek.

"Bless you, Mr. Parsons. Good night."

Iris let herself into the house. There was a light on in the hall, otherwise the place was in darkness.

"Matt?"

She called out her brother's name, and walked around switching on lights. Not by nature a nervous person, she nevertheless did not care to be alone in the house, and

63

particularly not in the dark. Since there was no doubt in her mind about her father's innocence, then it followed that the man who killed Ruby was still loose. He'd managed to gain access once before, and Iris liked to be able to see all around her.

" Matt."

Her second call was more from habit than expectation. He couldn't have gone very far, she knew, because the car was still in the garage. Since Matthew had passed his driving test a few months earlier, nothing would persuade him to walk anywhere more than a couple of hundred yards distant.

A cup of tea would be acceptable, she decided. The note was in the kitchen, propped against the kettle.

' Bored with my own company. Gone to help across the road. Have to start sometime.

M. Ellis—Corporal (Chip-Section)'

She smiled, and switched the kettle on. Then she had another idea, and switched it off again. This was an ideal opportunity. She retrieved her bag from the table in the hall, rummaged around for her key-ring. There was an unusual-shaped key on it, the end almost triangular. Then she went upstairs, switching on lights as she went, and looking in every room. She was quite alone. Going to the huge linen chest on the landing, she began to lift out sheets, blankets and pillowcases, piling them neatly beside her. At the bottom, lay the various sets of heavy curtains which would come in useful some day, but which had lain undisturbed ever since she could remember. They were more awkward to lift, but soon they too were in an orderly pile behind her. At the bottom of the chest lay a long, flat case, the sort used for certain musical instruments. Taking the triangular key, Iris sprang the lock, and lifted back the lid.

64

Inside, in orderly bundles, lay rows and rows of five-and ten-pound banknotes. Iris began to count.

*　　*　　*

The woman in charge of the archives at the *Daily Courier* was a brisk, dark-haired widow in her early forties. Ivy Trotman ruled all the library activities with a rod of iron, and was proud of having the best-indexed records in Fleet Street. She looked up, as a man tapped on the little glass cubicle which was her office, and came in, smiling at her.

" Hallo Trotters, how've you been keeping?"

A lot of the severity left her face as she inspected him.

" Well, well. Mr. Bradford, if memory serves, I'm fine, thank you. Are you? Where on earth have you been? You haven't been around interfering with my system for I don't know how long."

He frowned, realising she had not heard his story.

" No," he admitted, " I left the force, you know."

Mrs. Trotman was astonished.

" No, I didn't know. What's the story? I thought you were going to stay till they gave you the Commissioner's job."

" That was the intention," he admitted. " But I had a bit of a row. With the medical examiners."

Her sympathy was quick, and genuine.

" Oh, I can't tell you how sorry I am. Look, if you'd rather not discuss it—"

" No, no, it's all right. I'm not at death's door, or anything like that. It's just that I'm not quite fit enough for them to keep me."

She didn't believe it, but she nodded her understanding.

" Just as well then, perhaps, in the long run. You're certainly looking very well. Now, what can I do for you?"

Five minutes later, Jack Bradford was poring over the

newspaper reports on the murder of Ruby Ellis, nee
Masters.

SEVEN

After absorbing every scrap of information he could find
about the Ellis case, Jack Bradford paid a visit to the library.
There was still one hour to go before closing time, and he
wanted to use the excellent reference facilities. If Tony
Jervis was still in business as a photographer, one or other
of the information sources would provide the details.
Forty minutes later he closed the last volume with a small,
sigh and walked back along the shelving to replace it. Disappointed, he went out into the murky evening, and set
about finding a taxi to take him home.

He lived in Kensington these days, on the top floor of a
five-storey, luxury apartment block. It was a far cry from
the two-roomed flat in Balham, which had been his home
during his days at the Yard. Bradford had no dependants,
no one in the world to answer to, and he saw no reason
to stockpile money. Not any more. There had been a time
when things were very different, when every spare penny
was tucked gleefully away. But that was before Louise died.
After that, there hadn't seemed to be much point in anything, certainly none in hoarding cash. He'd gone a little
wild for a time, watched with some anxiety by his superiors,
but had gradually settled down. Not to normal, exactly, not
to being just as he was before. The recovered Bradford
was a harder man, more cynical, more world-weary, and,
if anything, an even better police officer than previously.

" Here we go, Mr. Bradford."

The taxi-driver spoke over his shoulder. Bradford opened the door, and got out. One of the small advantages of having been a Yard officer for years was that a lot of people got to know you, even if only by sight. He walked into the bright-lit warmth of the small entrance hall, watched by the careful eyes of the uniformed night porter behind the desk.

" Evening, Mr. Bradford. Turning chilly."

" Hello Cyril. Any news about my car?"

" I'll see."

Cyril turned to the bank of wooden pigeon holes behind him.

" Note here for you."

Bradford opened the folded sheet, and read that the routine service had been carried out, and minor defects corrected. The charge would be forty eight pounds fifty, and a detailed invoice would be forwarded through the post.

" Not too bad, I suppose," he muttered.

" Sir?"

" Nothing. This says the keys are in the desk."

" Oh, are they?"

Cyril opened a drawer, and rummaged inside, coming up with a small bunch of keys.

" Are these the ones?"

" No. Mine have a brown leather tab on them."

More rummaging, then the keys were in his pocket and he walked over to the open lift. At the fifth floor he emerged onto the carpeted landing and let himself into number twenty-seven. The sight of the expensive living room, with its soft and padded luxury, was still sufficiently novel to give him pleasure as the wall lights sprang to life. He grunted with self-satisfaction, and walked across to a well-stocked bar, pouring himself a glass of Macon from an elec- trically-cooled shelf. Bradford was a wine-drinker, and had by this time learned sufficient about wine to avoid the doubtful title of connoisseur, and to regard people who claimed it with resigned disapproval.

Carrying the drink across the room, he sank deep into an ivory leather chair, and pulled a telephone within reach. He dialled Directory Enquiries, and listened patiently to the brr-brr at the other end.

" Directory Enquiries. Can I help you?"

" Scotland Yard," he announced. " Let me talk to the supervisor, please."

"Just a moment."

A pause, then a calm, unflurried woman announced: " Supervisor here."

" Good evening. Scotland Yard. My name is Sergeant Hogan. We're hoping you can help us."

" We'll do our best, sergeant."

" We're trying to trace one of your subscribers. We have his name, and his profession, and we're fairly sure his premises were in the West End somewhere."

" Did you say ' were '?"

" Yes. That's the problem. Our information is nine or ten years old. I shouldn't have had to bother you, because we always used to keep your old directories. But we've had this drive for the last year, economising on space," his voice was scornful. " We've thrown away anything over five years old, so you're our only hope. The name is Jervis, Tony Jervis. He's a photographer."

" I see." The supervisor's voice was doubtful. " Nine or ten years, you say? I don't honestly know whether I could go that far back at this time of night. Could it wait till tomorrow?"

" The matter is urgent," he insisted. " Your computer people work all night, surely, unless my information is out of date."

" Very well. But it will take a few minutes. I'll have to call you back."

68

"No," he cut in sharply, before she broke the connection. "We're out pursuing enquiries at the moment. Could I try again in fifteen minutes? And whom shall I ask for, please?"

She told him, and he hung up.

One fine day, he told himself, people in different parts of London are going to get together, and set up a manhunt for this Sergeant Hogan. It was a name Bradford used frequently over the telephone. He glanced at his watch. In five minutes he'd be able to get a summary of the days's racing results on the radio. He switched on, and the stereophonic speakers filled the room with the dying minutes of a Czechoslovakian opera. Bradford turned down the volume, and waited. The music ground to a climax of triumphant discord, and faded mercifully away. An announcer, using the solemn tones reserved normally for State occasions, or the death of some prominent person, advised listeners that a repeat broadcast could be heard on Sunday morning. Bradford regarded this as a fair warning, giving people adequate time to make alternative arrangements. Then another voice came on.

"Here are today's sports results. And first, racing."

Jack Bradford was an inconsistent man when it came to horse-racing. Despite the knowledge he had of the inside world of the people involved, knowledge gained slowly in the course of his official duties, he still placed his regular bets with the same amateur enthusiasm as any duke or dustman. The tipsters and the form-guide experts were read more as gossip-columnists than as providers of real information. If Bradford had cause to travel on a particular day, and there happened to be a horse named Rail Ticket or Booking Clerk, he would regard this as personal information from the gods to himself. The fact that the horse had not won a race for two years, and was listed at fifty to one, he pushed to one side with blithe disregard. As a result, he lost consistently. The saving grace of his system was, that when one of his choices somehow contrived to labour past the winning post ahead of its rivals, the size of win would often be large. These occasional triumphs seemed to vindicate his whole methods, or lack of it, and he would happily resume his fortune-telling technique the following day.

The announcer advised him that he had not been successful on this particular day, and he switched off the programme, with mild disappointment. It was time for his telephone call. The supervisor was triumphant at being able to supply the information, and Bradford, as ' Sergeant Hogan ', thanked her profusely before replacing the receiver.

His pencilled note read: ' Jervis, A., 39 Cockpole Street W.1.'

It would be, he reflected. Cockpole Street was in Soho, part of the maze behind the upper end of Shaftesbury Avenue, and very familiar territory to him, as to any other police officer. Was there any point in going down there tonight, he wondered? He decided against it. Jervis was no longer there, and he would be unlikely to learn anything useful at that time of evening. It would wait till morning.

* * *

The next day, after opening up the office at Villiers Street, and ensuring that his familiar, comforting presence had been noted by the locals, he set out in search of Mr. Jervis.

The day had begun in a shroud of mist, but this had lifted slowly, as the sun gained strength. Bradford joined the hurrying shoppers as they poured up towards the Strand, bent on the urgent annual ceremony of leaving as much money in the hands of the shopkeepers as could reasonably be achieved by the end of the day. The walking man felt an odd detachment from the throng, because this was his town, and they were merely the human element necessary to give it flesh during daytime hours.

In Trafalgar Square, a patrolling constable recognised him, and gave a friendly nod across the heads of the shoppers. Bradford returned the greeting, and went on his way. He was in no hurry, and it was fifteen minutes before he turned into Cockpole Street. Number 39 was a bookshop. Not the kind of bookshop to be found in Charing Cross Road, a bare hundred yards distant, but a bright, cheerful place. Garish displays of lurid paperback novels covered every inch of space, and in a dozen different languages. The shop was already busy, with tourists well to the fore, as they stared and fingered, and jostled one another in the narrow aisles.

Bradford walked to the far end, where a small dark man was busily stacking new supplies of an Italian-language adventure story.

" You the proprietor?" he demanded.

The little man stopped work, and looked at him suspiciously.

" Yes. What can I do for you?"

" We are conducting certain enquiries about a former tenant of these premises. You may be able to help us."

The questioner was careful not to claim that he was a police officer. At the same time, he spoke as if he were, and he knew he had the requisite bearing. That, plus the use of the plural ' we ', was usually enough.

Certainly it was enough for the proprietor. He had recently had his own misunderstandings with the police, something to do with import licences for the goods on display. He hadn't understood it all, not entirely, but was very relieved to know that this new visit was not connected.

" Be glad to, if I can. Former tenant, you say? I think

she's still down in Brighton. Far as I know, anyway. I've got the address here, somewhere. Hang on, and I'll find it."

"Before you do that, you said 'she'. What was the lady's name?"

"Why, Mrs. Jackson, of course. Thought you'd know that."

The little man was worried now. If this policeman really wanted to know about Mrs. Jackson, it was funny he didn't even know her name. Odd, that was.

Bradford nodded patiently.

"I see. This may not be the person we're interested in. What did Mrs. Jackson use the premises for?"

You may well ask, thought the shop-keeper. He couldn't be from the local nick, this feller. They'd have told him quick enough. Some of the stories would make a man's hair stand on end.

Out loud, he said.

"Ladies' stuff, of course. Stockings, and underwear and that. You know, the usual."

The tall man shook his head.

"No. She's not the one. Must have been before her, then."

The proprietor frowned.

"Blimey, you are going back a bit. Years. I don't think I can help you."

"Well let's try. How long have you been here?"

"Two years. Well, three in March."

"And Mrs. Jackson?"

"Search me. Years, I think. Four years. Five. Perhaps more. I don't honestly know."

What was this, he wondered? Some kind of bleeding history test? How am I supposed to know all this stuff?

Bradford couldn't read his mind, but he could make a shrewd guess as to what was going on behind the worried face.

72

"Well, never mind," he soothed. "What about the neighbours? Anybody close by who's been here for a long time?"

The little man hesitated. You didn't go around setting the police on your neighbours. Not very nice, that wasn't. Still, if this geezer was going back years, it couldn't do any harm, really. He decided to take the plunge.

"You could ask at the caff. Three doors down. He's been here a long time. To listen to him, sometimes, you'd think he'd been here since the Great Fire of London."

Bradford grinned.

"Like that, eh? Well, he might be the very man for this enquiry. Thank you for your help."

He turned to go.

"Tell you what, officer."

The little man was smiling impishly.

"What?"

"Tell him you're trying to find out who started it."

"Started what?"

"The Great Fire."

The shopkeeper exploded into joyous laughter, which was infectious. His tall visitor was laughing himself, as he went back out into the street. The exterior of the café was not inviting. Woodwork, which had been white at some stage, was now peeling and stained. The windows were greasy and fly-specked, and an aged hand-written menu set out the usual fried assortment, all with chips. Well, somebody must eat in the place, otherwise how could the man stay in business? Bradford walked in, adjusting his eyes to the gloomy interior. A stooping, grey-haired woman peered at him through a cloud of steam.

"Yes?"

"Guvnor about?"

By way of reply, she dropped an evil-looking cloth on the marble counter and shuffled to the wall, where she lifted

73

a small wooden panel.

" Charlie. Visitor."

There was a muffled sound from the unseen Charlie.

" 'ow do I know? Come and ask him."

She glared at the visitor defiantly and went to sit on an old wooden chair in the corner. A curtain was pushed back, and a small, round man peeked anxiously in.

" You want me?" he demanded.

" If you're the proprietor, yes."

" What about? I'm not buying anything. Anything—at—all," he emphasised.

" Don't worry, I'm not a salesman. Want to ask you a couple of questions. Think you may be able to help us."

At the mention of questions, the old woman snorted, leaned her elbow on a shelf of cigarettes, and regarded Bradford with sullen malice.

" Questions? What sort of questions? Questions about what? Who are you?"

Charlie rattled off his own interrogation at machine-gun speed. People in Cockpole Street didn't like questions. And most people who came to the street wouldn't dream of asking any. This bloke was some kind of official. Some sort of busybody, that's what he was.

Bradford stared pointedly at the crone.

" It's rather private," he replied, patiently.

" Private is it?" Charlie hesitated. " Well, if it's private, you'd better come through, I s'pose."

" Thank you."

Bradford pushed the curtain aside, and stepped into the small back room. The only window was a disconsolate-looking square in the ceiling, which was firmly closed, and had probably been so for years. The proud owner of the establishment sat himself down in a faded armchair. There was a crate of beer within his reach, and a huge ashtray on a broken wooden table was full to overflow. The atmosphere was rank.

"To start with, who are you mister?" demanded Charlie.

"I'm making enquiries about a man who used to have premises in this street, some years back. They tell me you know more about the history of the street than anyone."

"Do they?" the fat man's face was crafty. "Well, p'raps I do, and then again p'raps I don't. Anyway, knowing's not telling, is it?"

Bradford recognised the preliminaries to a bartering session. He grunted, taking out his wallet, and looking inside it.

"I could easily find out by taking a taxi round to the landlords, but I don't want the trouble. The taxi would probably cost what? Two quid, say?"

"Plus your time," augmented the other. "Valuable, that is, I shouldn't wonder. More like five quid."

Bradford's smile was very thin.

"You're forgetting. I could just pick you up and slam you against the wall," he suggested. "Wouldn't cost me a penny then. But generosity has always been my weakness. Three quid, and start talking."

The listener's greasy face had been pallid before. Now it was white. In his world, there were talkers, and doers. Charlie knew a doer when he saw one.

"No need to get nasty," he spluttered. "Little matter of business. What do you want to know?"

"Number thirty nine. Bookshop. Used to be a ladies' underwear gaff."

The fat man looked unhappy. If this geezer wanted to talk about Mrs. Jackson, he was going to be unlucky. There were people involved there. Big people, who'd soon know how to sort out this clever bastard, big as he was.

"I sort of remember," he admitted. "Vague, though. It's a long time back."

Bradford was thankful not to be interested in the mysterious Mrs. Jackson. She was obviously an interesting woman, and Charlie was all set to develop a bad memory, where she was concerned.

He shook his head.

" I want to go further back than that," he announced. " Back to a man who used the place as a photographic studio. Man named Jervis. Tony Jervis."

Charlie's face cleared at once.

" The queer? Yeah, I remember him. Blimey, you really are going back. Must be ten years."

" Nine or ten," agreed the tall man. " What sort of a man was he? Was he really queer, or is that just an expression?"

This brought a snort of derision.

" Oh, he was queer all right. Queer as a coot. Mauve trousers, silk shirts. Quite a sight, I can tell you. Still, at least they could trust him with the birds."

Progress, thought Bradford, with quiet satisfaction.

" Birds?"

" S'right. He done all the pictures for outside the night clubs, and that. They all used to come down here. Little darlings, they were. Hundreds of 'em. In them days, it was nothing to have a cab pull up, and four or five of 'em get out. Used to liven the place up a bit, you can stand on me."

" I can imagine. He was in a fair way of business then, I gather."

" Making a bomb," Charlie nodded sagely. " On top of the show-business lot, this Jervis was doing naughties as well. For the dirty books, you know what I mean? These days of course, it don't mean nothing. You can buy 'em in the tube station, can't you? But it was different, then. Bit under cover, if you follow me."

Bradford was beginning to think his money would be

well spent.

" What sort of age man was he?"

The reply was instant, and positive.

" He was thirty seven."

Bradford raised his eyebrows.

" You seem very certain, after all these years."

" Well, I would be, wouldn't I? Remember all that, clear as a bell."

" Mind telling me why?"

Charlie's voice was almost patient.

" It's obvious, isn't it? Not every day one of the neighbours gets himself scragged."

" Scragged?"

" Yeah. You know. Murdered."

EIGHT

" Wait a minute, Paddy. Wait."

The tall spare man called out softly, and the golden labrador halted obediently, looked round, and squatted on its haunches. If the boss said wait, he would wait. If he said run, then he would do that. Anything the man said was all right with Paddy. There was a deep affection between these two, and they were a familiar sight on their twice-daily walks across the common. Paddy knew why they were stopping. His man usually paused by this particular tree. Something to do with that thing he carried in his mouth.

Former Detective Superintendent Tunstall used the tree as a break against the light winter breeze, and set about lighting his pipe. There weren't a great many advantages about retirement, so far as he was concerned, but one of them was being able to light a pipe in peace and quiet, and being certain of smoking it without interruption. Pipes and police work are uneasy companions, the unpredictable break periods being more attuned to a few quick puffs on a cigarette.

He looked at the dog, sitting patiently on the grass, and smiled. Couple of old 'uns together, that's what they were. Just as well, too. He doubted whether his arms and shoulders these days would be equal to the task of controlling the powerful animal Paddy had been, a few short years before.

" C'm on boy. Missus'll be getting the coffee going about now."

Paddy ambled ahead of him, sniffing automatically at the grass, but his real attention was focused on a group of small boys up ahead, who were kicking a ball about. Paddy liked to play with balls, and if this one happened to come his way, he would make off with it, and the boys would have to chase him for it.

The dog had no way of knowing that his master was thinking along the same lines, but with a difference. The former police officer was thinking that, not so long ago, Paddy would have joined in with the boys, and stolen the ball from under their feet. Now he waited for the ball to come to him. A sign of old age. Unconsciously, Tunstall began to walk more briskly at the thought.

Ellen saw them coming from the kitchen window, and switched the kettle on. Jim always looked forward to his coffee, after the morning walk. He made a bit of a mess sometimes, when he returned, particularly if it had been raining. But Ellen never complained. She was only too thankful to see him taking his proper exercise. She heard the terrible stories about some men who'd retired. Getting up at all hours, slopping around the house in their dressing gowns. Not bothering to shave, or take a proper interest

78

in themselves. That wasn't Jim at all. He was up, washed and breakfasted, and out of the house by nine o'clock most days. He did not intend to sit around, waiting for a fatty heart to catch up with him.

" Coffee's just about ready," she announced, as the back door opened. "And please wipe that dog's feet."

Paddy knew she was talking about him, but he didn't mind. The missus was a bit of a fusspot sometimes, turning him off comfortable chairs, and pushing him out of the bedrooms, but she was all right, really. He stood patiently on the coconut mat, while the boss wiped mud off his feet with an old cloth. Then he bounded into the corner, making loud slopping sounds as he dipped his nose into the water bowl.

" Any post?" demanded Tunstall.

" Nothing exciting. Something from the Post Office. Looks like a reminder."

" That'll be the telephone bill. I'll pop in this afternoon and get it settled."

" Hang your coat up love, and go and sit down. I'll bring your coffee in."

" Right."

He went through into the comfortable sitting room, and parked himself in a favourite chair. A moment later, Ellen came in with a small tray.

" Oh," he noticed, " are you drinking yours with me, for a change?"

" Yes. We're having a pie for lunch, and it's already in. So I've got a few minutes to spare."

" Good."

She sat down opposite him, stirring at her coffee. The real reason she was sitting with her husband was because she had a nice surprise for him, and she wanted to share it.

" Had a telephone call, from a man."

" Oh, yes. What man?"

" He said he was one of your team once, for a short while."

Tunstall was all attention at once.

" Did he, though? What name?"

" Bradford."

" Bradford, Bradford," muttered her husband.

Ellen gave him a chance to remember without prompting, then said:

" He said it was the Greenwich Warehouse case. He was a sergeant at the time. They put him under you because it would be one of the last opportunities he would have of seeing how you worked. He was very young, at the time."

The Greenwich job. Yes, he remembered it very well. Bradford?

" Tall, dark chap? Curly hair."

Ellen smiled patiently.

" He was on the telephone dear, not the television."

" H'm."

Tunstall got up, and went over to the little mahogany bureau, unlocking the lid so that it fell forward to complete a small desk.

Inside were a pile of neatly stacked folders. He riffled through them, selected one, and opened it, beginning to read. After a while, Ellen said:

" Your coffee's getting cold."

" M'm? Yes. Yes."

He took the folder back to his chair, swallowing the coffee obediently before resuming his study.

" Yes, here he is. Mentioned him twice. He was the officer who tackled that b— that blighter Williams. Jigger Williams. Bloke took a swing at him with a crowbar, but Bradford went for him regardless. Yes, of course I remember him. Good copper. Listen to this. ' Sergeant Bradford, in addition to his physical courage in tackling the suspect

80

Williams, acted throughout with great discipline, coupled with intelligence, and a keen interest in the overall conduct of the case.' That's what I said."

"I didn't know you wrote reports on everybody, after a case was finished."

"No, no," he explained patiently. "Bradford was detached to me, to see how he would get on. What I had read out was a memo I sent to his own guvnor when he went back on his normal duties."

"Ah."

"Well come on, Mrs. You've kept me in suspense long enough, even for you. What did he want?"

"Now, let me make sure I get this right. He said he'd come across something, which connected back to an old case of yours, and he'd like to talk to you about it."

"What case?"

"He didn't say."

"Well, didn't you ask him?"

Ellen noted the sudden asperity in her husband's tone, and smiled inwardly. He was back at work already, to listen to him.

"No dear. I'm sorry, I didn't think of it."

"Have to phone him back, I s'pose. Where is he, at the Yard?"

Now was her big moment.

"I don't know. I asked him whether it would take very long, and he said well, it could. So I said why didn't he come down here for lunch? Then you could both talk as long as you like."

Tunstall's impatience evaporated.

"Did you, by George?"

"Yes. I thought it would be a nice change for you."

"It will. It will, indeed."

He smiled. It would be a nice change for Bradford too, he reflected. A decent, home-cooked lunch in a private house, wasn't part of a working copper's normal day. What could he want? It would have to be important for him to take—what?—three hours away from the job. What could be that important?

* * *

Jack Bradford turned into the road, and drove along slowly, checking the house names on the left hand side. He was looking for Poplar Cottage, which ought by rights to have at least one tree giving the name some authenticity. When he found the house, there was one tree, but it was an oak. He pulled the white Jaguar to a gentle halt, and climbed out. The front door of the house opened at once, and there was the legendary Chopper Tunstall, waiting for him.

He smiled down the path, as he closed the gate carefully behind him.

"Hallo, guvnor. It's been a few years."

Tunstall held out his hand.

"It's Jack, isn't it? Jack Bradford. Come on in. I'm very pleased to see you."

Bradford followed him into the neat, orderly house, and was soon sitting in a comfortable chair.

"Could manage a beer, I expect?"

He didn't want to drink beer, but he recognised the need to be hospitable in the retired man.

"That would be fine, guvnor."

When they both held a glass, Tunstall said:

"Well, cheers."

"Cheers."

The beer was cold, and bitter.

"Now then, what do we have to call you these days? Not quite chief super yet, I suppose?"

"Not quite," he grinned.

This was part of the conversation he hadn't been

looking forward to, at all. Still, it had to be gone through. He told the story, being careful to outline a fair amount of detail about his work, and his progress, before reaching the hard part. Tunstall listened eagerly, asking questions about old colleagues, as the story went on. When Bradford reached the end, and told him of his medical problems, he was properly sympathetic.

"That's bad luck. Bloody bad luck. When was all this?"

"Eighteen months ago. Just over."

The former superintendent clucked his tongue.

"Yes, but wait a minute, you're supposed to be down here on a case. How do you make that out, then?"

Bradford steeled himself.

"I'm a private investigator. Being a copper is the only thing I know, only thing I ever wanted to do. If I can't be one on the force, then I decided I'd have to go it alone."

Disappointment was plain on his listener's face. Bradford was not surprised. He'd expected something of the kind. The old warhorse had thought the Yard couldn't manage without him, had to contact him after years of retirement, to help them out. Now, as it developed, he was only being sought by a private operative, and his opinion of the breed was no higher than that of most official policemen.

"H'm. This puts a different light on things," said a disgruntled Tunstall. "I mean, my knowledge, such as it is, is not really private to me, you know. What I know, what I've learned, has all been as a Yard officer. Sort of within the family, if you follow me. Official. I feel free to talk quite openly with any serving copper. Family business, you see. But as to discussing police business with an outsider—well—"

Outsider. The word hurt Bradford more than he would have expected. Technically, it was true enough, he admitted. But he didn't feel like an outsider, didn't want to be outside. It wasn't his fault if—just a minute, he checked himself. You're starting to feel sorry for yourself again. We're supposed to have left all that behind us. Aloud, he said:

"I can understand your position, and I respect it. But the thing I'm talking about happened ten years ago. It's not a question of mucking up an investigation or anything like that. The case is long closed."

"Is it?" queried Tunstall, shrewdly. "You're here though, aren't you?"

"Look. Let me put it like this. I'll tell you what's going on. You can decide whether helping me is a starter or not. I shan't make any fuss. If you say to me, no, that's confidential police business, even after all these years, then I shall respect what you say. Does that sound fair?"

Tunstall thought about it.

"The way you put it, I suppose it does, yes. All right. You talk, and I'll listen. Then we'll see."

Bradford unzipped his flat leather case, and took out the least offensive of his three photographs.

"I'm trying to trace the girl's movements. Ten years ago."

His host took the picture, and looked at it impassively.

"Not exactly the one to take to the vicar's tea-party, is she? Who is the girl, and why are you checking on her?"

"The name is Masters, Ruby Masters. There's a widower who wants to marry her. He has a daughter, a grown-up daughter, and she's not very keen on the idea. The woman Ruby seems quiet enough now, quite respectable. But the daughter isn't satisfied. She searched through her stuff, and found this picture. She's hired me to look into it. It may be harmless, it may not. But she doesn't want her father to go getting himself tied up for life to a bad lot."

"I see. Why don't you just tackle this Ruby?"

The visitor shook his head.

84

"Wouldn't do at all," he demurred. "If the father found out that his daughter had hired me, there'd be hell to pay. The girl doesn't want it out in the open. And she's trying to be fair, too. If Ruby made a few mistakes years ago, that's understandable, and no more will be said. But if she's a rank outsider, then the balloon will go up."

"Yes. That makes sense. But look, where do I come in? I mean, I may have seen the girl at some time. I haven't the faintest idea. Seen hundreds like her. Arrested a few of 'em, too. What's the connection?"

Bradford leaned over and pointed to the name, printed in the corner of the photograph.

"He is. The photographer. I thought I'd start with him. See if he kept his old records, that kind of thing."

Tunstall was peering into the indicated corner. But he knew he'd have to confess.

"Can't read it," he admitted. "Haven't got my glasses on. Never used to wear them, you know. It's only lately."

The questioner nodded.

"You'll remember him, all right. Jervis. Tony Jervis."

"Ah."

The older man let out a sigh, and settled back in his chair, thinking. The photograph lay, unheeded now, beside him.

"So that's how you got on to me?" he said, finally.

"Yes. When I found out he'd been murdered, I went and looked up the story. It made a hell of a splash at the time. I could even vaguely remember bits of it myself."

"Vaguely? Had you joined the force, then?"

"Only just. I was still a cadet. Still trying to learn the Judge's Rules, when this happened."

"Son, I was still learning the Judge's Rules up to the day I retired."

They exchanged grins.

"So you read up the case, and thought you'd come

85

here. Why?"

"It seemed to me very odd. There's only one lead to Ruby Masters' earlier life, and that man was murdered. I thought if I could contact some of the other people who knew him, did business with him, I might find somebody who'd remember the girl."

"Bit thin."

"It's all I have."

"Well, you know the basic facts. This Jervis was a fairy. Jerve the Perve, everybody called him. He was working late one night in his studio in—in—"

"Cockpole Street."

"—that's right. In Cockpole Street. Somebody came in, somebody he seems to have been expecting. This somebody shot him. Killed him. I was never able to pin it on anybody."

Bradford's eyes gleamed. When a police officer of Tunstall's standing uses that kind of phraseology, it usually means that they knew who was responsible, but hadn't anything sufficiently concrete to bring into a courtroom.

"But you know who it was?" he queried. "Or you had a pretty good idea."

Tunstall heaved his shoulders in resignation.

"You know what it's like. There are cases where you know perfectly well what the answer is. Everybody else knows. Sometimes even, I've known this to happen, even the villain knows that you know. And he knows damn well there's bugger all you can do about it. This was like that."

He stared at the wall opposite, lost in private thoughts.

Bradford said gently,

"If you don't give me at least half a tip, guvnor, I'm right up a gum tree. Jervis was my only hope."

The ex-superintendent looked at him through heavy-lidded eyes.

" If you aren't careful, you're in danger of starting me off on my favourite subject. Once I start, I go on for hours."

" I'll take a chance." Bradford spoke without hesitation.

" All right."

Tunstall went over to his little bureau, and unlocked it. From the interior he removed a file. It was much thicker than all the others. He opened it at random, stroking the page abstractedly.

" Don't say you weren't warned, Jack," he said lightly. " And don't expect any sympathy from any of the Yard lot, once you tell them you got me started on my subject."

" What is your subject, guvnor?" queried the eager Bradford.

The standing man waved the file, and half-smiled.

" The Great Bullion Raid."

Bradford settled down.

NINE

The robbery at the much-vaunted Eagleton Warehouse had captured the imagination of press and public alike. Originally, descriptions of it varied from the inevitable ' Crime of the Century ' to ' Pirates of the Air ', but finally it earned its place in the crime annals as the Great Bullion Raid.

The planning, the timing, the effrontery, and in the end, the sheer simplicity of the whole venture had been clasped fervently by Fleet Street, and the press of the whole world. Here was a big story, with all the elements dear to the hearts of the pressmen, and to the public.

The warehouse was the pride and joy of the security people at the docks. It had been designed and constructed from the point of view of impregnability first, and storage requirements second. This made it unique. The usual order of priorities was the other way round. The vast sheds were normally made suitable for their prime purpose, which was, after all, storage. When this requirement had been satisfied, security arrangements were added on afterwards. Weak spots were identified, and special attention given to making them secure. For ninety per cent of the traffic, this approach had proved adequate enough, and the success percentage was high enough to satisfy even the doom-mongers of the insurance world. But with high-value, easily disposable cargo, there was always added risk, and it was in this area that the war between the security forces and the villains continued. The chance of successful raiding was always slim, but it existed, and where there is a possibility of easy pickings, there will always be desperate men willing to risk their liberty.

The designers of the Eagleton Warehouse had analysed all existing security systems, together with attempts by criminals, successful or otherwise, to circumvent them. Steel fences, dogs, television cameras, floodlighting, electronic devices, steel doors, every anti-theft measure in use was listed and studied. The finished building was simplicity itself. A straightforward square of concrete, the lowest windows thirty feet above the ground. The only gap at ground level was that afforded by the doors, massive electronically controlled sliding doors, which locked on a timing mechanism every night, and were thick enough to withstand the assault of anything short of a military tank. Man-dependant security at street level was non-existent. There were no watchmen to be attacked, no guard posts to be duped by false uniforms or documents. Analysis had shown that the main weakness of all precautions lay in two areas. The first, and by far the weakest of these, was people. People were vulnerable to attack, threats, bribes, and, in the last resort, death. The second area was devices. Elaborate, expensive devices, which were capable of performing amazing and intricate tricks. These were vulnerable in two major respects. They could be rendered inoperative, all too frequently, by the simplest action, such as the removal of a fuse, or the breaking of a connection. The other weakness lay in the fact that people came to believe implicitly in their strength. Nothing could go wrong if the magic box was switched on, and months of experience of the truth of this assumption would eliminate gradually the human edge, the need to be satisfied, the checking. Failures would occur, or be induced, and there would be no emergency alternative which could be brought into effective operation in sufficient time.

The Eagleton planners knew all this. So, instead of adding more devices, more people, thicker concrete, they quite simply scrapped the whole conception. There were no people waiting to be banged on the head, no devices to be overcome. Nothing at all. Would-be intruders could approach the walls with impunity, because there was nothing they could do when they arrived. Fifty feet up, a catwalk surrounded the warehouse, and this was patrolled at irregular intervals, by men whose only task was to stare downwards into the lighted area, immune from any form of attack, and report any untoward happenings.

Everything was controlled at roof level. Heating, air conditioning, radio contact with police, and the comfortable working quarters of the four men on watch. It was the ambition of every security officer to obtain one of these highly paid, safe jobs, in the most advanced warehouse in Europe. The Eagleton Warehouse was impregnable.

Until the Great Bullion Raid.

It was the year of the Thames Pageant. Much planning

had gone into this event, and it was to be a twenty four hour spree for London, and the expected one million tourists. The river would be floodlit for the whole length of its London wandering, and procession and carnivals would be organised throughout the whole of the day and far into the night. It was to be a no-expense-spared binge, aimed at bringing the river to startled life, and providing a huge shot in the arm for the London image, along with an inflow of money on a big scale. Most of the expenditure would come from public sources, because of the patriotic nature of the venture. Most of the income would go to private sources, because of the venal nature of man. But there was no doubt, this was going to be a binge to be remembered, and the whole of the capital city entered into it with gusto.

The Pageant was big news, and the television news agencies were keenly alive to this. For a month before the event, the public were whetted by previews, interviews, inside information and general gossip about the coming attraction. Preparation for the three-hour torchlit procession of barges and floats made the river a hive of industry, greater than it had known since the eighteenth century.

To the criminal fraternity, it was only natural that such an event should bring prosperity to all. Everyone would be out looking for a good time, anxious to spend their money. They would throng the streets, the bars, the restaurants. The police would be stretched to the limit, and beyond, in trying to control the crowds, and preventing the city from clogging up entirely under the human invasion. Movement of police traffic would be difficult, and nigh impossible in the more congested areas. It looked like being a great day for crime.

The burglars, pickpockets and the smash and grab artists prepared themselves for a spree of their own.

So too did a small group of determined and ruthless men, who watched and planned in a tight-knit, tight-lipped conspiracy of their own. At that time they were unknown to the public at large. Soon, each one would be a national figure, though that was no part of their plan, or wishes. For these men, from the day of the Pageant until the day they died, would always be known as the Great Bullion Raiders.

The actual raid was simplicity itself. The weather had been kind to the organisers of the Thames Pageant, and the dying sun at nine o'clock that evening glowed redly over a happy London. The greatest of the organised events, the river procession itself, was just beginning. London shook off the tiredness following a carefree day, put on a fresh shirt, and settled to the business of enjoying the long night.

There were four helicopters in the night sky, packed with cameramen and reporters, representing all the news media. They swooped and hovered, darting here and there to present some new aspect of the magnificent scene spread out below them. The pilots paid little attention to the pageant, being far more occupied in keeping close radio contact with each other to avoid any risk of collision, and scanning the night sky with the same nervous agility as a fighter pilot. One of them was quick to spot the stranger, a large military type of helicopter, which seemed to be rather too far back from the dock area for the taking of good pictures. He warned his fellow-pilots of the new arrival, and tried to make radio contact, but without success. Then he nudged one of the cameramen.

" Bloody sightseers," he grumbled. " See 'em?"

The cameraman peered across the sky and nodded.

" Looks as if he might be in trouble," he said. " He's going down, look. Quick Max, get a shot of that chopper. Over there. Might be a bit of a scoop for us."

He was more prophetic than he realised. Max was able to record for posterity the actual carrying out of the Great Bullion Raid. Not that he nor anyone else realised it at that moment.

The strange helicopter dropped down towards the roof of the Eagleton Warehouse. A rope ladder was slung overboard and men descended rapidly to the flat tarmac covering.

"I think he's in trouble," reported Max, still filming. "There are men getting away from the machine. No sign of any panic, though. Seem to be quite orderly."

"Keep on it," advised his companion. "It might blow up or something."

On the roof, away from the gaze of the unsuspecting Max, one of the men unscrewed a cover from an air vent. Two others came forward and began to drop small canisters inside. The cover was replaced, and a piece of thick blanket secured over it.

The three men in the working area had no chance. One was already asleep, spending his two-hour break catching up on the rest he had lost while celebrating the pageant earlier. One man was at the radio control desk, the other sitting in an easy chair, reading a newspaper. The gas filled the small room in a matter of seconds, and they both fell deeply unconscious. They saw nothing of the masked figures who appeared, and began to tie their hands and feet.

"Bloke missing," grunted one.

"Be on the catwalk. He'll come in through that door there. Tell Lou to wish him good evening."

When the unsuspecting guard returned from his patrol, he was beaten senseless and tied up like his colleagues.

In the news helicopter, Max said:

"He's lifting away."

The pilot nodded.

"Must have overdone it. Took too many passengers, I

92

expect. Got a little bit of trouble, fuel perhaps. Now that he's lighter, he can get away, and deal with it. Not exactly front page stuff, is it?"

Inside the Eagleton Warehouse, sweating cursing men were manhandling gold bars up to the roof.

"These bleeders don't half weigh," grumbled one.

"Should hope so," replied another. "That's a Rolls Royce at least, you've got there. Ever carried a Rolls Royce on your own before?"

The idea of translating the gold into everyday terms caught the fancy of the rest.

"One hundred birds, all to meself."

"Two thousand bottles of scotch."

And so they continued. On the roof, the pile began to mount. One man surveyed the scene.

"Spread 'em out," he ordered.

"Eh?"

"Spread 'em out," he repeated. "This is a roof, not a factory floor. That weight will break through here like a stone through a bleeding window, if we don't spread it."

They did as he said, and the work went on. Thirty minutes later there was a roar in the sky.

"He's coming back. That's it," announced the leader.

"Come on Mac, there's plenty more yet," protested another.

"And that's where it stays," said Mac, nastily. "That's a helicopter we've got. Not a bleeding oil tanker. I know exactly how much load he can carry, and that's it. Now, get up that ladder and start passing the stuff. And remember this. All of you. That pilot is in charge. He knows exactly where he wants these goods. Otherwise it'll wind up in the bleeding sea. Don't argue with him."

The work of loading began.

"Hello," announced Max. "He's back."

"Who is?" queried his partner half-heartedly.

"The chopper who had the trouble before. I think he's picking up his passengers again."

"Big deal. Look, down there, that's the Bounty, a complete carbon copy of Captain Bligh's old ship. What a lovely sight. Close up on that one as much as you can, Max. A lovely shot, there."

*   *   *

Jack Bradford listened, absorbed, as he heard the story summarised by one of the few people who were really in the know. So much had been written and said about the raid, there had even been a major movie, and a six-part television series produced, that the average man thought he knew all about it. For once, Bradford would have to class himself as an outsider. Detective Superintendent Tunstall had spent two and a half years on the case, and even at the end of it, Bradford was still a very young detective-constable.

"Amazing," he said. "Absolutely amazing. Was the film of any use? The one the BBC chap took?"

"Oh yes. It was invaluable in many ways. It fixed the time to a second, for one thing, it showed us the actual helicopter, for another."

"And the men taking part. You could actually see them climbing down the rope ladder."

Tunstall sighed.

"Ah yes. We could see them, all right. But identifying them was a different matter entirely. They were too far away, and it was half-dark. We were able to work out approximate heights and builds, of course. In the end, we got 'em all. Well, except those two in South America. We know where they are, and who they are. They can't move an inch. Might as well be in the nick."

"Could you tell me a bit about the money side? What does a man do with all those gold bars? I mean, I'd know a couple of places where I could drop one, or even two. But in that quantity, I wouldn't know where to begin."

"That was one of our big troubles. Gold is just gold, wherever you take it. It doesn't have pound signs or dollar signs, or any other signs on it. It's just gold, and it's viable currency anywhere. The gang got away with a million and a half, that night. We finally worked it out that they settled for half price, somewhere near the Franco-Swiss border. That's three quarters of a million. By the end, we had recovered over six hundred thousand. It wasn't bad, considering. We reckon there's a hundred thousand with the two villains in South America. So there was fifty thousand we finally couldn't account for. I don't think that's bad, do you?"

The listener shook his head.

"I think it's a bloody marvel, guvnor. I really do. And I know you personally went after the thieves, one by one."

That was all Tunstall needed to start him off again. This time he led Bradford through each chase, each capture. And, of course, the trials.

"The Mulloy brothers, Mac and Joe, they got eighteen years apiece. Sid Carpenter got sixteen. You won't remember Sid. Boxer, he was. Light-heavy, back in the sixties. Nice fighter, but he could never finish. Saw him at the Albert Hall, once. Anyway, he went sour after that, and played quite a part up on that roof. Then there was Freddie Price. He got twelve. Always been a bit of a nuisance, Freddie. Very quick-tempered. Good looking bloke, always around with the talent, you know. But too quick with his hands. Lou Reisman, he was another one. I always maintained Lou was one of the leaders, but the judge thought otherwise. Only gave him four years. Then, let's see—"

He went through the whole gang, plus the various people who'd been connected with the crime, either before or after the event. Bradford didn't want to interrupt him, because he had no way of telling which part of the historic puzzle might fit into his own jigsaw.

" It's a lovely story," he said, at the end. " And a lovely piece of detection, if I may say so, with respect. But you haven't referred to my man yet. Jervis. He has to fit in somewhere, because it was him who got you started on the story."

A thick finger wagged at him.

" I was coming back to him, Jack. The plan was, after everything was over, all these blokes were going to skip. They did, too, most of 'em. We picked them up all over the world, as you know. Every man had a false passport. Lovely jobs they were. Cost one thousand pounds apiece, and you couldn't tell them from the real thing. That was your friend Jervis' contribution. Ten passports, ten thousand quid. By the time we got around to details of that kind, Jervis was dead."

" And the money?"

" Never turned up. Jervis wasn't my concern, really. Murder Squad were dealing with it. But they were very helpful, when it turned out there was a connection with the bullion job. Just as well, really, because I don't think they'd have come up with the answer, but for that."

" But you said the case wasn't solved," objected Bradford.

" No, I didn't, Jack. Didn't say that at all. I said there was no trial. It was Freddie Price killed Jervis. We just never could pin it on him. He used to grin at me, even after I nailed him for the robbery, whenever I raised the subject of Jervis. ' Prove it, Mr. Tunstall ', he'd say. ' You get on and prove it.' And of course, I couldn't. No fingerprints, no witnesses, no motive, even."

" No connection with the fact that Jervis was queer?"

" I tried that. Price laughed till he cried. He'd get me

twenty women, he said, fifty if I liked. They would all tell me how queer he was. I knew it was true, too. So, as I say, there was no way it could be brought to our Freddie's doorstep. Anyway, he collected twelve years. Give him time to think about it. Come to think of it, he's about due out."

Ellen Tunstall put her head around the door.

"I'm sorry to interrupt," she announced, "but if this food is kept waiting one minute longer, I will not be responsible."

Bradford leaped to his feet.

"My fault, Mrs. Tunstall. I talk too much, I'm afraid."

Her eyes twinkled as she looked from her tall visitor to the man in the chair.

"H'm," she said, and went away.

"Better get in," muttered her husband, rising.

"Yes. One question, super. You wouldn't let me borrow your file, would you?"

Tunstall shook his head.

"No, lad. Sorry. I won't let that out of my sight. Tell you what, though. If you'd like to spend an hour going through it, after lunch, make a few notes, you could do that. Have this room to yourself. Nobody'll disturb you."

Bradford grabbed the offer.

"Thank you. I'd appreciate that very much."

As he passed the window, he remembered the oak tree.

"Tell me, why Poplar Cottage? There isn't a poplar in the whole road."

At the open door, Tunstall chuckled.

"Obvious, isn't it? My first station that was. The old Poplar nick."

97

TEN

Detective Superintendent Robin Morgan glowered at the report in his hand. Despite his popular nickname, he was feeling anything but cocky this particular morning, as he studied the unwelcome bulletin for the third time.

Picking up the telephone, he barked:

" Sergeant."

" Sir."

" Find out whether Inspector Barnett is on the patch. I want to see him."

" He's just phoned sir. He's on his way to see you."

" Oh. Good."

Joe Barnett had already heard then. Amazing, the way the drums beat in these headquarters. A few minutes later, there was a knock at the door, and Barnett came in.

" Sit down, Joe. You've heard the news, then?"

Barnett had heard some news, that's why he was here. But with his chief, he was always cautious.

" News, sir?"

" From up North?"

" No sir. What's happened?"

Morgan glowered.

" What's happened, inspector, is that a large quantity of stolen goods has been discovered. On an articulated lorry that started out from Bristol with a normal half-load. Pure chance, almost. One of the lorry's indicators was defective. The local people had had their suspicions about this particular driver for some time. This gave them an excuse to stop him, and they hit the jackpot. Just north of Manchester."

He waited for this to sink in. Barnett nodded.

"From Bristol, you say? So the transfer of goods took place somewhere between there and Manchester."

"Obviously," said the super, tersely. "They have asked our Regional Crime mob to sniff around at this end. Copy to me for information."

He waved the offending paper.

"Copy to me for information," he repeated nastily. "You know what it means, I imagine? It means they're telling me, in a nice way, that they've rumbled some villains who've been carrying out crimes on my patch, and what a pity I didn't catch 'em myself."

Barnett shifted uneasily.

"We don't know it was round here, sir," he pointed out. "Could have been the Midlands. Anywhere."

"Do you remember a little chat we had a few weeks ago?"

It was typical of Morgan, when he was in one of these moods, to throw an unanswerable question at people. He and the inspector had had dozens of little chats in the past weeks.

"Which particular chat, sir?"

"The particular chat where we talked about that café in the Ellis murder. Walt's or something. We said we'd be keeping a little eye on it. Doesn't seem to have done much good, does it?"

Morgan was being unfair. He knew it, and his listener knew it, but the only way to deal with him was to let him get it out of his system. To contradict him, or make excuses, would be a mistake.

"Looks as though we missed them, all right," returned Barnett regretfully. "Who was the driver, sir? Do we know him?"

Unwittingly, he was touching the sorest spot of all.

"Know him?" replied the super, in his most dangerous, light-hearted tone. "Oh yes, we know him. Half the coppers in the world know him. By name, at least. Lou Reisman, that's who it was. Only one of the Great Bullion Raiders. No one of consequence. He comes in and out of our patch, as he pleases. 'Morning, Mr. Reisman. Nice weather we're having. Had any good tickles lately, Mr. Reisman?' I expect our patrol people salute when he goes past, eh?"

Now that he knew the villain's name, Barnett could sympathise with the old man's feelings.

"Pity we missed him," he admitted.

"Inspector, I am not a vindictive man," and Morgan eyed him, to see whether his face showed signs of disagreement, "but I want you to look into this. Go through all the daily reports, interview the duty officers. If you can find any dereliction, particularly where this so-called surveillance on Walt's Café is concerned, I shall have somebody's arse in a sling."

"Right, sir."

It was a dismissal, but Barnett stayed in his chair.

"One other thing sir, if you've got a minute."

"Well?"

"In a way, it's almost connected. Still in Walt's Café, only this time it's about the murder case."

The famous eyebrows shot up.

"Thought it was all done and dusted. It had better be. The trial is only a few weeks away."

"I'm sure it is, sir, but there's been a little development. Ellis has a daughter, you'll recall, name of Iris."

"And?"

"Sergeant Hammond went to London, shopping, the other day. On his way home, he saw the girl go into a building in Villiers Street. She visited a private investigator, by the name of Bradford. John A. Bradford."

Morgan became interested.

" Did she, though? What about?"

Since he couldn't answer the question, Barnett disregarded it.

" This Bradford is the president of an organisation called the Small Traders Mutual Trust. When I heard that, I got very interested. You had told me to keep an eye on the possible theft of goods in transit at the café—"

—a snort—

" —and it seemed to me there might just be a connection. If the man Bradford dealt with a lot of small business people, he might be on the retail end of the goods. He'd certainly have enough little firms to choose from."

The superintendent wagged his head up and down. The inspector had his full attention now. Perhaps it would be possible to salvage something from this Reisman debacle. Aloud, he said:

" I hope you've not been doing anything foolish, Joe. You haven't been poking around in London, have you? The Met'll go spare."

" No sir, certainly not. But I ran a check on Bradford. Put him through the machine, to find out whether we had anything on him."

" And—"

Barnett looked discomfited.

" He turns out to be one Jack Bradford, ex detective-inspector, New Scotland Yard. Retired on ill-health grounds, just over a year ago. A grade one, first-class copper, commendations up to his ears."

" Ill health could have been an excuse, to get rid of him."

" Not this time, guvnor. He was only twenty eight years old—"

—twenty eight?" Morgan's interruption was disbelieving.

"—twenty eight, sir. That's how good he was at the job. He was a great loss, up there, it seems. The answer I got to my enquiry wasn't exactly snotty, but it wasn't over-polite, either. Jack Bradford, Jabber in the trade, was, and is, very highly regarded."

The super stared at the wall.

"Twenty eight," he muttered. "All right, so where does that leave us, inspector? You seem to have caught a cold on the stolen goods angle."

"Frankly sir, it leaves me bothered. We know a bit about Miss Ellis. Nice girl. Why should she want to see a private investigator? It occurs to me—"

"—it occurs to you, inspector, that the girl may know something about her step-mother's murder that we don't know. Am I right?"

"It's just a shot in the dark, sir. But with her father's trial coming up—"

He left the sentence unfinished.

Morgan frowned, as he digested this new thought. His earlier annoyance was forgotten now, as he gave proper professional attention to what could evolve into a serious matter.

"I don't like it," he announced finally. "Do you want to go and see the girl? Tackle her about this?"

Barnett hesitated.

"I'm thinking about the trial, guvnor. We don't want the defence counsel shouting about police harrassment of the accused man's family."

"Agreed. Well, let me have a report, anyway. There's a bit of time in hand. Won't hurt to let it stew for a day or two."

*　　　*　　　*

"Icy? Can I come in?"

At the sound of her brother's voice, Iris sat upright on the bed, putting down the paperback novel.

" Yes Matt, come on."

The door opened, and Matt's cheery face appeared. He grinned apologetically.

" Sorry to disturb you."

" That's all right, I was only reading."

It was a half-truth. For the past twenty minutes she had been staring, unseeing, at page fifty three of the book. It had taken her the greater part of a fortnight to get even that far, and her recollection of the first fifty two pages were very vague.

They were very close these two, and drawn closer than ever by the events of the past few weeks. In a sense, the experience was akin to the one they'd suffered together ten years earlier, when they lost their mother. This time, they had lost a new mother, and for all practical purposes, their father too. Not that their father's absence could be anything but temporary, they were quite convinced of that. But it was a conviction of wishing and hoping and loving, without basis in any roots of fact or evidence. For the first few days, they had spent the whole time in argument, discussion, theory about the murder. Gradually, they had talked themselves out, as the normal pressure of routine living claimed their attention. Neither of them had mentioned it now for some time.

Matt was carrying some papers, whch he now placed on the dressing table. Then he lifted a pile of newly-ironed clothes out of her armchair, looked around uncertainly for a new resting place.

" Put them on the end of the bed for now," she suggested.

He did that, and sat himself in the armchair. Matt was looking tired, she thought. It wasn't good for a young man to spend such long hours in the atmosphere of the café.

"Been doing some sums," he announced. "Very interesting."

Matt's natural aptitude for figures was a long-standing mystery to them all. It was not a common family trait. Iris had slaved at her mathematics, in order to achieve a barely respectable pass at the 'O' level examination years before. Then she had heaved a great sigh of relief, thrown her text books into a cupboard, and never given the subject a further thought.

"What kind of sums?" she queried. "And keep it simple, Matt. You know how quickly I get lost."

He grinned, and seemed to change the subject.

"Dad said I could do it, when I saw him on Tuesday."

"Do what?"

"Have a go at the books."

"But surely, Mr. Jenkins—"

"That's what Dad said at first. But I pointed out that Mr. Jenkins charges a fee every time he comes. There's no telling how long this—this situation will last. If we're going to be running the place for any length of time, then we can't do it blind. We have to get to grips with the simple arithmetic of things."

"Yes. I suppose so."

It was an unwelcome thought. Iris recalled, without pleasure, the long sessions in the kitchen every month between her father and Ruby. They were very meticulous about keeping the books straight. She didn't look forward with any relish to their places being taken by Matt and herself.

Matt chuckled at the expression on her face.

"Don't worry, Bumps, I'm not going to put you through it. I've done it all. Forwards and backwards, several times. There's nothing to it really, once you apply a bit of system. What I've got here," and he tapped at his papers, "is the finished article. Unfortunately, I don't like it."

Iris was relieved to know that her contribution was not going to include sorting through masses of paper.

" Don't like what?"

" The end result. We've been losing money ever since Dad went away."

" Losing? I don't understand. The café always seems as busy as ever."

" I know. That's what makes it odd. Oh, and when I say losing, by the way, I only mean we're making less profit. We're still in the black. But we're two hundred pounds short. Roughly, I mean. Give or take a few pounds."

She was relieved at the size of the problem.

" Two hundred? In roughly two months. But that could be just a drop in the takings. Increase in food costs. And, don't forget, Dad's away. We've had to get the odd stranger in. Could be a bit of pilfering."

Matt shook his head.

" I've been through everything. Naturally, being new, I've been extra careful. Taken a lot more trouble than people usually would. I've been going back over what Ruby and Dad were doing, done all their work again. And that's why I'm worried. I don't agree with their figures, either."

Iris was puzzled now.

" But they've been doing it for years," she protested. " You're not suggesting they've been wrong all this time, and now suddenly you're right? I don't want to hurt your feelings, Matt, but if that's the situation, perhaps just one visit to Mr. Jenkins might explain it. It would be worth his fee to have our minds at rest."

He was not smiling as he shook his head.

" I don't want Mr. Jenkins involved, Icy. This conversation has to be strictly between you and me. This might not do Dad any good at all."

Iris said carefully:

"You'll have to explain that. In simple terms."

"I told you I've been to a lot of trouble. Checked everything. Prices we charge, fuel bills, supplies bills, the lot. Since Dad went, the profit we're showing in the café is about right."

"But you just said—"

"Wait a minute. The profit is about right, on a supplies in and out basis. Using exactly the same methods, I know that the profit in the past has always been about a hundred pounds a month higher than it ought to be."

"But Mr. Jenkins would have queried—"

"No, he wouldn't. That's the point. His job is to check the figures he's given. Make sure they're honest, and can be supported by paper work. He doesn't set the prices or anything. So, if the profit is high, he simply thinks to himself how well they run the place, how above-board the whole thing is."

"But the income-tax man—"

"He's happy. He's not worried about people who declare income. He's worried about people who try to hide it."

Iris chewed at her lower lip, an old habit from childhood. All she understood so far was that her father and Ruby were more efficient at running the place than they were. It seemed natural, indeed proper.

"Well come on, you've got something to say. You don't want Mr. Jenkins. So you must have a reason. And you're worried. Why?"

Her brother's face was very clouded now.

"There's profit which has been declared from that café, going back as far as I can, which never came from there. About a hundred quid a month. Where did Dad get it? Where did it come from?"

Iris was all attention.

"What are you saying? That Dad's been on the fiddle?

Is that what you're saying?"

"I don't know what I'm saying, Icy. I'm just telling you the facts."

Her mind was racing now. Matt was suggesting their father could have been involved in something crooked. It was unthinkable. With her natural dislike for figures, she kept telling herself that Matt was wrong. He had to be. With the best will in the world, and no matter how clever he thought he was being, he had to be wrong. Her father, dammit their father, couldn't be—. But there was the money. Matt didn't know about that. Could it be that— No. No. And she couldn't tell him, that was the worst part. If there was guilty knowledge, then it was hers. It wouldn't be fair to involve Matt. Not until it was absolutely unavoidable.

Her mind was spinning, and her brother's anxious face watched her closely. She had to stop this. Stop it now. What was it her old form-mistress used to say? Ah yes. When in doubt, do nowt.

"Matt, I don't know what the answer is, obviously. But I think you're right, that we have to be very careful about this. As you say, nothing that can harm Dad must come out. Let me make you a proposition. It's early days. How would it be if we stick to your system for one more month? That can't hurt anybody, and it might help. There might be some unexplained factor, something neither of us has thought of, which may become clearer, given another few weeks. If it does, well and good. If there's nothing, then we'll know you're right. We'll be no worse off than we are now, and we'll be more certain of our facts. What do you say?"

He was clearly relieved. When he'd come into the room, his mind had been in a turmoil of speculation, about exposure of who knew what kind of dark corners. Good old Iris had come up with a sensible, reasoned answer.

"I like it," he announced. "I'll watch every farthing during the next month. Twice."

"Good," she grinned. "Shall I make a cup of tea?"

ELEVEN

Many times in the past, when Jack Bradford had been nearing the end of an investigation, he would experience an odd excitement. Weeks, and sometimes months, of painstaking enquiry and routine checking, would bring him to a point where he suddenly knew he had the solution. What had been inanimate became all at once alive, the impersonal became personal, and this strange sensation would come over him. His more experienced colleagues knew the feeling, and had a mundane expression for it.

"He's got a good sniffer, young Bradford."

His sniffer had come to life when he was poring over Jim Tunstall's exhaustive file on the Great Bullion Raid. The Mulloy brothers, who had been the masterminds behind the robbery, ran a business as haulage contractors. Besides themselves, there were three other drivers, and the honest side of the business was a profitable, going concern. Their legitimate income was supplemented by the occasional fiddlings of cargo, and all the men had records either of minor convictions, or had at least come under the eye of the law more than once. The Mulloys wanted their own men on the big job, people they knew and trusted. Two of them, Freddie Price and Lou Reisman, had been willing volunteers, but the third man had cried off. His name was Tommy Freeling. He was no angel, and by no means above a spot of routine thieving, but the very size of the Mulloy scheme was too much for him. After weeks of argument, it was agreed that he would be left out. Freeling could have been in a dangerous position, since he possessed knowledge that could have jeopardised the scheme, both before and after it was carried out. But he was fortunate, in that his sister was married to one of the brothers, and he had a long record of reliability when it came to keeping his mouth shut.

He had been caught up in the net, when enquiries began, and given a most thorough grilling by the investigating team, but they came gradually to accept his story, and let him go, with reluctance. He, together with Price and Reisman, had been a devil-may-care easy money man for years. It seemed a pity not to be able to put him in the bag, along with the rest. But his innocence was transparent, and his alibis for all relevant times quite unshakable.

At first, Bradford had not been very interested in Freeling. The man he wanted to learn about was Freddie Price. Price, he learned, had been released a few weeks earlier, and had returned to his old London haunts. It wouldn't be too hard to find him, but Bradford was not yet ready for that. Price was a hard case, and unlikely to be shaken easily by questioning from an unofficial source. It was Jim Tunstall's view that Price had killed Tony Jervis, and if that assumption was correct, then the man would be just as wary now as on the day of the crime itself. No, the best man to question would be Lou Reisman.

A lesser member of the team, and not as bright as some of the others, he had been a free man for some years. Reisman had not been at all reluctant to talk to the pressmen, after his release, and had even appeared on television a couple of times. There was always someone writing a new book about the Great Bullion Raid, and willing to pay out a few pounds to talk to one of the participants.

Unfortunately for Bradford's intentions, Reisman was

once again in the hands of the police. He'd been up to his old cargo-thieving tricks again, so that avenue was closed for the time being. Pity he'd been pinched up North. It would have been a nice coincidence, if the Wessex Regional squad had nabbed him. Preferably in the forecourt of Walt's Café, with the gun that killed Ruby Ellis still in his pocket. Bradford grinned to himself, at the thought of how nice and tidy that would make everything.

That left the third member of the trio, Tommy Freeling. His knowledge of the big robbery was only second hand, and if that crime had been Bradford's main interest, he would not have bothered with the man. But he wanted background information about Freddie Price, not necessarily because of the robbery, and for that purpose Freeling had known him as well as anybody.

It was a very well-situated house. Good solid residential area, with neat well-tended gardens, and a general air of prosperity. Bradford parked the car, and walked up the path to the cheerful yellow door. The door chimes played the first notes of an old nursery rhyme. The visitor stood back, so that anyone checking from a window could get a good look at him.

The door opened and a man inspected him carefully. Tommy Freeling was ten years older than his picture on the file, but he still retained some of the lurking devilment on his face.

"Good morning," said Bradford pleasantly. "Mr. Freeling, isn't it?"

The other man didn't answer at once. He kept on looking at the man on the doorstep, his eyes flickering occasionally to the car parked in the road. Eventually he spoke, and his tone was not friendly.

"Your name's Robert," he said flatly. "I can tell 'em a mile off."

Bradford realised that the bluff approach was not the

right one. He wiped the smile off his face.

"Now, now Tommy," he said quietly. "I'm doing you a favour, as it is. Nice, plain motor car, nice civilian suit. Your neighbours can't tell me a mile off, can they? If you'd sooner have uniforms, and a nice white car with blue stripes on it, so they'll know what's going on, then we'll have to see what can be done."

Freeling considered this.

"What do you want?"

"Little chat, Tommy. That's all. Shall we go inside? People next door will start to wonder why you're keeping me here, in a minute."

Tommy Freeling hesitated, then stood back.

"Why not? I haven't done nothing. But not long, mind. I'm going out."

Bradford went into the small, bright hallway, and waited. The door was closed.

"Better come in here."

The small sitting room was a riot of colour. A startling orange carpet was set off by light blue walls, and a black ceiling. The imitation-leather suite was off-white. The set-pieces, carefully displayed, were a massive television set, a shiny cocktail cabinet, and enough stereophonic equipment to meet the requirements of an average town hall. On the facing wall, a flight of orange and blue ducks chased each other towards the ceiling, in a desperate attempt at escape. Bradford could sympathise with the ducks.

"Very nice, Tommy. You're very comfortable here."

"It cost enough," said Freeling sourly. "And I've got receipts."

"I'm sure you have, sure you have. Don't get the wrong idea, I'm not here to cause you any trouble."

"What do you want, then? They don't send Yard blokes out of London to smell the country air."

"Mind if I sit down?"

Without waiting for an answer, Bradford parked himself on the edge of one of the heavy, over-stuffed armchairs. The unwilling host sat well away, over by the door.

"Your old friends are out and about then, Tommy."

"Old friends?"

"Lou Reisman, for one."

"Lou's been out for years. Seen him once, on the box. That's the only place I've seen him. He hasn't been here."

"You sure?"

"Course I'm sure. I'm finished with all that. Years ago. Straight, I am. Dead straight. Why don't you ask at the local nick? They know me."

Freeling's protest was calm, and assured. It wasn't the sweaty calm of a man with a good alibi, but the deeper calm of the man who has nothing to hide. An experienced investigator learns to identify the distincton.

"Lou's being a bad boy again," said Bradford, deliberately.

Tommy Freeling's face was unmoved.

"So what?"

"So he's been taking things, things that don't belong to him. You'd think he'd know better by now. Naughty boy."

"Better talk to Lou, then."

"Oh we are, we are. Got him dead to rights. Whole lorry-load of the goods."

Freeling was puzzled.

"Why tell me?"

The visitor smiled.

"Well, you know Lou. Bit careless, at times. There's a few bits missing. You know what tidy minds we have. We want to find it all."

"I don't understand this, at all. I haven't even laid eyes on Lou for, let's see, ten years. Yes, it must be. My little Tommy wasn't even born, the last time, and he's nine. Why

112

tell me?"

Bradford shrugged.

"You know how people are. Some coppers just can't help remembering things. Like your name, for instance. Keeps cropping up. I'm not like that, at all. Live and let live, that's my motto. Do you know, some people even wanted to search your house? I'm against it, personally."

The seated man watched him closely.

"There's nothing here," he said flatly. "Tell you what I'll do. You got a warrant?"

"No. This is just a chat."

"So you say. But I'll tell you what. You can search the place. Now. Without a warrant. I can't say fairer than that."

He leaned back triumphantly. Tommy Freeling wasn't standing on his dignity. He didn't need to. He was an innocent man.

Bradford shook his head.

"No, I couldn't do that. It wouldn't be legal."

"Huh," Tommy snorted. "That'll be the day, when you let that bother you."

"No, it would have to be legal. Proper warrant, two cars, siren. Asking all the neighbours if they've noticed anything. Have a chat with the local publican, the shop-keepers. How do you pay your bills? All that. You know the sort of thing."

Freeling's face was white.

"You'll ruin me. All for nothing. I'm well-known round here. People like me. Just an ordinary bloke, like them. My kids grew up here. They don't know nothing about the old days."

"I know," said Bradford, regretfully. "I'm doing all I can to stop it. You might be able to help."

He looked across at the worried face.

"Help? How can I? I told you, I don't know nothing

about Lou. It's the truth, Gawd help me."

" Not about Lou. Let's talk about Freddie Price."

The worried look was joined by puzzlement.

" Freddie? I haven't even thought about him since they dropped a big 'un on him. Don't tell me he's at it again. He's still inside."

" No. Our Freddie's been out a couple of months now."

" Go on. Remission, I s'pose. Yes, that would be about right."

" That's the problem, you see. Until we picked up Lou, a couple of days ago, all you cowboys were loose at the same time. Lou, and Freddie and you. Just like the old days."

" Balls," ejaculated Tommy, " what are you on about, the old days?'

" Well, let me explain it to you. You used to do a bit of thieving. Here and there, odds and ends. It's all on the files. The long-distance game. It's still going on, you know. That's what Lou's been up to. Freddie's in it, as well. Only we can't find Freddie. But we can find you."

Beads of sweat had broken out on Freeling's brow. Innocent he may be, but he knew how much trouble could be caused, if this quiet, unemotional bastard put his mind to it. All his efforts, years of building a decent life, could all be swept away, his good name ruined, his family life shattered. He couldn't understand why they would want to do it to him. What would they gain?

" Look Mr.—"

" —Bradford—"

" —Mr. Bradford, you want to make me sweat, all right, I'm sweating. I don't see what's in it for you. All these threats, and that. I'm not worried about your suspicions. I'm innocent, and that'll be proved. It's not that. It's the family. My kids, my job, everything."

His tormentor nodded solemnly.

"I know, Tommy. Believe me, I'm on your side. I think it would be a terrible thing. I'm going to stop it, if I have my way. But you'll have to help me."

A flash of hope appeared on the worried face, then went.

"How can I help you?" he said dully. "I don't know nothing."

"I think you might, even if you don't realise it. Freddie's only been out a little while. He hasn't had time to build up new connections. So we're checking all his old ones. You could help us there. And don't worry about anybody finding out. It won't go beyond this room."

"Don't suppose I can remember—"

"You'll have to try. It's the same old game, you see. Back on the long-distance jockey lark. Some people have no imagination. Lay-bys, cafés, the same old routine."

"What about his sister? He had a sister, in Chingford."

"We've got people watching there," lied Bradford, smoothly.

"There was an old auntie, too, down by the seaside somewhere."

"The old girl is dead. Three years ago. What about his girl-friends? He had a few of those, in his time."

Despite the tension in the room, Freeling grinned quickly.

"Right bastard, Freddie was. Had 'em all over the place."

"Yes, but special ones, Tommy. One he went back to now and then. On the all-night runs. Plenty of the lads have a regular piece on regular trips. Try to think."

"Dear me."

Tommy closed his eyes, thinking.

"There was one just outside Glasgow. What was her name? Annie? No. Edie. That was it."

Bradford took out a notebook.

"That's the kind of thing we need. Tell you what. Perhaps it would help if you did it systematically. Think about the big routes, all the stops. Pretend you're back in the old waggon, and just drive along, looking for your next cup of coffee, the next meal. That'll get your memory working. Start in Glasgow, with this Edie. What was the name of the place?"

The suggestion was sound. Tommy Freeling visualised himself, back in the driving cab, radio blaring, a few cans of beer within reach on the floor. He remembered the steady flicking of the wiper-blades, as the eight-wheeler droned through the night, saw again the welcome distant light-haze of the nearing café. Could almost smell the frying bacon, the smoke, the steam rising from wet duffle coats. He began to talk, and Bradford scribbled dutifully away. Most of this would be of no use to him, but he knew that direct questions might well produce blank responses. By getting Freeling to relive the driving routines, he was hoping something valuable would emerge. He had covered four pages of notes before the speaking man had arrived at the Bristol area.

" Walt's, that was it. Place called Great Fording. Dunno why they called it Great. Couldn't imagine anywhere smaller. There was a bird there, I remember. Bit special, she was. Quiet little thing. Not like some of the others. Common lot, if you follow me. This one was, how would you put it, respectable somehow. I'll get the name in a minute. I can see her face."

" Was it Ruby?"

Tommy Freeling had been holding his head in his hands, and staring at the floor, with the effort of concentration, but now he looked up, puzzled at the question.

" Little Ruby," he said, nodding. " D'you know, I'm so busy thinking about the driving, I almost forgot about Ruby. You know about her, then?"

" We know something about her, not much."

" Well look, could we come back to her in a minute?

116

Finish what we're doing? This one down there, at the café—"

Bradford's pencil froze on the pad.

" Not Ruby, then?"

" No, no, no. I've got it. Margaret Ann, that was it. Tell you why I remember. It's the film star's name, see? The other way round. Ann Margaret, the film star. Only this one was Margaret Ann, see what I mean?"

" Yes, I see what you mean." Bradford drew a thick ring round the name, and added a question mark.

It was several minutes later, plus a potted history of a once-celebrated Bristol lady known as Seaport Susie, that they were able to get back to the matter of Ruby Masters.

" I always liked her," remembered Tommy. " Not the usual old brass at all. But once Freddie got his hands on her, she didn't have a chance."

" She got away in the end, though," Bradford reminded him. " What made her run off like that?"

Freeling shrugged.

" Search me. You'd have to ask her that one."

The investigator frowned. It almost sounded as though this man didn't realise that Ruby was dead.

" I would have done, if I'd found her in time. Ruby is dead, Tommy."

A small shadow appeared on the other's face.

" Little Ruby? Dead? You sure?"

" There's no doubt at all. Didn't you know about it?"

A shake of the head.

" Haven't seen her for—what—ten years. I'm sorry, though. What happened to her?"

Bradford was even more puzzled.

" Don't you read the papers? They made enough fuss about it."

" Go on. No, I don't get much time for the papers. I been working on the oil rigs this past year. Work and sleep, three months at a time. Real hard graft. I'm off again next week. Pays for this lot, though."

" I see."

That made sense. It also meant that Tommy Freeling was completely out of touch with developments.

" You didn't say how it happened," prompted Tommy.

" She was murdered. Her husband shot her. It was weeks ago now."

" Husband? She did settle down then. Glad about that. Now the bastard's done her in, eh? Well, well."

" Matter of fact," Bradford chose his words carefully, " the local police had a bit of trouble tracing her past history. She'd dropped right out of sight. Looked as though she meant to disappear, almost."

" Can't blame her for that. Did it meself."

" So you did. Do you happen to know why she ran away? The reason I'm asking is because she lived at Great Fording, of all places. Funny coincidence."

" Yeah."

Freeling got up and walked over to the window, staring out. There was a brass candlestick on the sill, with the figure of a clinging monkey either side of the base. Hideous.

Bradford waited. Freeling's laugh was unexpected.

" Funny innit? The way things happen. People get worked up, all excited, big dramas going on. A few years go by. None of it matters a fart, after all. Like Ruby, Freddie Price, the Bullion Raid, the lot. Then she winds up getting carved up by some yokel."

" I hadn't realised she was involved in the Bullion Raid," the seated man said, carefully. " Her name was never mentioned."

Freeling still kept his head turned away.

" Well she wasn't, not really. It was that time, though. You know, a coupla days before. When she buggered off, I mean."

" No, I didn't know that."

The one-time villain looked at him then.

" Poor little cow. Dead, eh? Well, it can't do no harm any more. I'll tell you what happened. It was me got her away."

" Really? Away from what?"

" From Pricey. She come to me one night, shaking like a leaf. Had a case with her, all packed. She said he was going to do for her. She had to get away."

Bradford lit a cigarette, trying to control his features.

" Why would he want to hurt her?"

A shrug.

" Who knows? He could be a vicious bastard when he liked."

" But you believed her? You thought he would kill her?"

Freeling gave a humourless smile.

" Not really. Mind you, he'd mark her for life, if he felt like it. Put her in the hospital. I've known him to do that before now. Still, she thought she was done for. Wanted to get away. Somewhere quiet. Anywhere. Somewhere nobody would ever find her. I couldn't take her very far. Tell you the truth, I was a bit boracic at the time. There was no extras, you see. All the lads were busy on the bullion job, and they weren't talking to me anyway."

" So you hadn't much money?"

A brief laugh.

" You could say that all right. I had just what petrol there was in the tank. I could have borrowed a few quid, but people might wonder why. And, on top of that, if Pricey was looking for her, there was no time to hang about."

" What did you do?"

Tommy scratched his head.

" Tell you the truth, she came to the wrong bloke. I

can tell you where it's all going on. The lights, and the gambling, and the birds, and all like that. But I don't know nothing about quiet places. I took her down to the only place I could think of. That little village there, behind the café in Great Fording. Best I could think of. Dumped her in the local pub for the night, and went home."

" And that was the last you heard of her?"

" Till today. Funny old world, innit?"

Funnier than you know, thought Bradford.

TWELVE

Iris got up from her chair with a snort of impatience, and switched off the television set. She hated war films anyway, and this one was distracting her thoughts. That is, if the disconnected whirling inside her head could be distinguished by such a title. She picked up a cigarette and lit it with a match, placing the spent wood carefully in the ashtray, where the last cigarette still smouldered.

According to her watch, it was two minutes past eight, and Jack Bradford had agreed to arrive at eight o'clock. Why couldn't people keep to time? If eight o'clock was too early, he should have said so. It was only an hour and a half from London these days, and it was three hours since they'd talked on the telephone. He'd wanted to come at once, but she had fixed the time. She didn't want him in the house until Matt was safely engaged on his nightly stint in the café. Her business with Bradford was something she had decided to keep from her brother. There was no point in upsetting him, with all this probable wild-goose chase about Ruby. Time enough for him to know, if anything ever developed.

And it seemed as though something may have. The investigator had been very cagey on the telephone, but that was to be expected, in these days of wire-tapping, and so forth. Though who would be interested enough in her affairs to do such a thing was a mystery. Well, whatever it was, the attractive, personable man whom she'd come to think of privately as 'her copper' had thought it sufficiently important to justify a trip down from London. The reason for her agitation was twofold. First and foremost was the exciting prospect of some development, anything which might be remotely useful in helping her father to prove his innocence of this ridiculous charge. Secondly, there was the opportunity of seeing Jack Bradford again. The tall man, with his good looks and obvious competence, had made an impression on Iris, when she visited him in his office. That had been his ground, and in working hours. She was on her own territory now, and eight o'clock in the evening was hardly working time.

Perhaps she ought just to check her hair again.

It was almost ten past eight when Bradford turned the wheel and entered the forecourt, getting his first glimpse of Walt's Café. He was annoyed at being late, annoyed at the impatient idiot who had pulled out recklessly to overtake an L-driver, and caused a collision which had blocked the road for a quarter of an hour. Bradford hated to be late. It went against all his training and his instinct. Apart from which, he was impatient to see the delectable Miss Ellis again. Strickly speaking, he admitted, he could have asked his only real question over the telephone, but then he wouldn't have seen the girl. Besides, he assured himself, there was really some justification for the trip. She couldn't look at photographs over the telephone, could she? But it was a thin consolation. There was little prospect of any success in that direction, and he knew it quite well. No, it had to be faced. He wanted to see Iris.

Iris Christine Ellis, he mused. It sounded better with the middle name included. Of course, the initials did form the word ice. Funny how some parents didn't give a thought to things like that. And they couldn't have done anything more misleading. Bradford was no stranger to women, and there was nothing glacial about the worried girl who'd come to his office.

Business must be thriving in the café he noted, threading his way through the neatly-parked heavy goods waggons. He drove around the side of the building, and into the much more brightly-lit area at the rear, pulling up outside the gate. Then he climbed out, lifting his brief-case from the seat, and locking the door carefully.

Nice-looking house, he decided, pressing on the bell. Of course, it was a murder-house now, after Ruby's death. In a small community like this, it would be a murder-house for the rest of its days. In twenty years, the locals would probably say it was haunted.

Iris opened the door, and looked at him speculatively.

"I know I'm late, and I'm sorry. There was an accident."

There was quick concern on her face.

"Accident? Oh, I hope—"

"No, no, not me. Some lunatic in front of me. But it took us quite a time to push all the rubbish off the roads."

He stood there, waiting. Iris recovered herself.

"Oh, I'm sorry. Please do come in, Mr. Bradford."

They went into a comfortable sitting room, and the visitor was quick to note the heaped glass ashtray.

"Can I get you a drink? There's usually some scotch, if that's all right?"

"Thank you, no. I don't drink spirits. They don't agree with me."

She liked his being in the room. Liked the confident presence in these familiar surroundings. It seemed to her

122

to be right, somehow. Oh Lord, he was waiting for her to say something again. She wasn't doing this very well at all.

"Please sit down, won't you, Mr. Bradford?"

He paused, and said:

"I wonder whether you might call me Jack? That would give me an excuse to call you Iris."

She smiled then.

"I will, if you'll sit down. You're making me nervous, filling up the whole room."

After they were seated, they both produced cigarettes at the same time, and laughed.

"Same brand, too," she commented. "Well I've got more than you. And a whole café full of them, just over there."

There was a slight tension in the air, a man-woman tension, and each of them was well aware of it.

Bradford spoke first.

"Miss Ellis," he began.

"Well, that didn't last long, Mr. Bradford." Iris placed heavy emphasis on the 'Mr.' and they both laughed.

"Sorry. Iris, then, I've been having quite a time with your step-mother's photograph." In a sense, he was regretting the loss of protection afforded by the more formal greeting. He was going to have to be very careful how much he told this girl. There was no need for her to be upset more than was necessary, for one thing. And he didn't want her to know things which might put her in danger, for another. "It was the photographer that put me on the track, originally."

Her eyes widened.

"Fancy him remembering her after all these years. Was she famous or something?"

He'd started badly.

"Perhaps I didn't word that too well," he amended. "I

123

should have said, it was my investigating the photographer that started it all. He's no longer in business, you see. The man is dead. Been dead for years."

She nodded, without understanding.

" But in that case—"

" However, I talked to people who'd known him. He was mixed up in some rather shady deals, our Mr. Jervis. When I dug around, I found that there were some people he knew, who had a direct link with this place."

" Great Fording?" she asked, puzzled.

" No. With the café. They were lorry drivers, and this was one of the places they used."

" Bit tenuous, isn't it? There are hundreds and hundreds of people in that category. Especially when you go back so many years."

Bradford had decided from the outset that he was not going to mention the Great Bullion Raid, unless it was absolutely necessary. Not that the girl could know anything about that. She could only have been, what, twelve or thirteen years old when it happened. But that didn't exonerate the father. Whether he'd murdered his wife or not, was one thing. But there was fifty thousand pounds still unaccounted for, and if Walter Ellis had any guilty knowledge about that money, Bradford was not going to give anything away which might serve as a warning to him. Not even for this one, lovely as she was.

Now, he said:

" That's true. But not very many of your customers have police records, like these two. They knew Ruby Masters in London, and they used to call in here. Not quite so tenuous, would you say?"

Iris nibbled at her lower lip.

" All right. But where does that get us? I mean, all those years ago—"

She stopped talking, waving her hands vaguely.

"If that had been the end of it," he told her gently, "I wouldn't have made the trip. As you say, it was years ago. But look at it step by step. The café, the two drivers, who have criminal dealings with Tony Jervis. Tony Jervis takes photographs of Ruby Masters. Ruby Masters knows the two men. And some time later, Ruby turns up in Great Fording. Before we know where we are, Ruby and your father are married."

The fair head was bent, as Iris followed him carefully. "But I don't see what you're driving at," she queried. "The way you put it, everything sounds sinister. As though there was something odd about the marriage. And I can tell you, here and now, they loved each other, those two. Ruby was a good woman, a good wife, and a marvellous step-mother to Matt and me. What are you saying?"

He shrugged. He didn't know the answer to that, himself. It would have been easily explained if some good-time girl had taken the café proprietor for a quick ride, and relieved him of his cash. Say, inside a year or so. But to settle down to a quiet life for eight or nine years did not jell with that kind of explanation. No, it seemed almost beyond question that the marriage had been genuine. A true partnership. But there was still money missing. And, the big and, Ruby had been murdered. Perhaps this was the time to try out his photographs.

Iris watched the capable hands unzipping the leather case. This had something to do with the money. All the money, she was sure of it. That case upstairs, which had been kept successfully hidden from Matt and herself. For how long? Years? It could be. And by whom? By Ruby, now dead, to whom it would no longer matter? Or by her father, accused of murder, and whose case would not be helped by the sudden discovery of a cache of stolen money? For there was no doubt in her mind that it was stolen. They were new notes, unused, and there were too many for it to be otherwise. And then there was the bribe-money, the hush money, or whatever it was. The hundred pounds a month that Matt had discovered when checking the books. These were things she had to keep to herself, keep away from this attractive, dangerous man. For that was what he had become, suddenly. A danger to her father's safety.

Jack Bradford produced two photographs. They were both from newspaper files, and much more natural than any he would have been able to obtain from police sources.

He stared at Lou Reisman's impudent grin, then at the defiant, more arrogant face of Freddie Price.

" You were trying to understand what connection there could be between what happened ten years ago, and the present day. This man here," and he touched Reisman's picture, " is a certain link. I'm not too positive about the other one, not yet. But this man was in the café recently, and he's been arrested again in the last couple of days. For theft. Big-scale theft, of cargo. The kind of cargo that is parked outside in your forecourt, at this very moment. Tons of it. Do you know him?"

Iris looked at the face, held it away, brought it close again.

" No. I couldn't swear to it, but I don't remember him at all."

Bradford was disappointed.

" You're quite sure?" he pressed.

" Well, I couldn't take an oath, but I'm fairly sure."

" Oh." Without much hope, he handed over Price's picture. " What about this one?"

Iris looked at Freddie Price, and didn't like him. He was handsome enough, almost too handsome. But there was something in his face, a hardness, perhaps. But something. She knew the type. There were women in plenty who would make a beeline for Freddie Price, and live to regret it. Cruelty, that was it. A kind of offhand, almost unthinking, cruelty.

"No," she said, positively. "I would remember him, I'm quite sure. And I don't like his face. But I've never seen him before."

That left Bradford with only one last card. A question he could have easily asked over the telephone, if he hadn't wanted to see this girl again.

"Back in those days," he began, "there was a woman who lived in the village. Could even still be here, for all I know. But there was a connection between her, and this one." He tapped at the Price portrait. "All I know about her is that her first name was Margaret. Margaret Ann somebody."

"Hello, got a visitor, have we?"

Matt stuck his cheerful head around the door. They both looked round.

"Oh, hello Matt. This is—er—a friend of mine, Jack Bradford. Jack, this is my brother Matt."

Bradford rose, and the two looked at each other. They shook hands.

Matt was embarrassed.

"Blimey, I seem to have put my foot in it. Sorry, Icy. Didn't realise you had a proper visitor. One of the customers said he thought he saw a police car, and I thought—well—I don't know what I thought, really."

He finished lamely, thinking he'd interrupted a very different kind of occasion.

Bradford realised at once that Iris had kept their business a secret from her younger brother. No harm in supporting her.

"That's all right," he laughed. "My own fault, for driving a white Jag. Bit flashy, really."

"Oh no," Matt disagreed. "Nice motor-car. Very nice. What's up, Icy? I know I'm a bit untidy, but you look as if you've seen a ghost."

Iris smiled distractedly.

"Nothing like that. You startled me, that's all."

Matt was even more convinced he'd put his foot in it. Anxious to change the subject, he spotted the photographs.

"Hello, what are these then?" He looked at the two glossy prints. "Wait a minute. Good grief, I just said you look as if you'd seen a ghost. Now, I think I am. Where on earth did this come from?"

He held one of the pictures out to Iris, who looked helpless.

"Why? It's nobody we know."

"Course it is. Well, you wouldn't know. You never did. It was all a big secret. I'd nearly forgotten him myself. But this is such a good likeness, I can see him now. Hear him laughing."

"Who is it Matt?" asked Bradford quietly.

"Well, it's Uncle Freddie, of course. I always promised I wouldn't tell. And I never did, you must admit. Never told anybody, not even you, Icy. Used to give me fifty pence, every time I saw him. It was a secret, you see. Because Dad didn't like him. But he was Mum's only cousin, wasn't he? Didn't do any harm for him to pop in when Dad was at work."

"Cousin?" echoed Iris flatly.

"Yes. I only found out myself by accident. Woke up one night, feeling a bit sick, and went looking for Mum. Uncle Freddie was here."

Bradford hardly dared to breathe.

When Iris spoke, her voice was harsh.

"Sit down, Jack. And you, Matt. There. We are going to have to talk."

"I'll have to get back," Matt argued. "The café—"

"Sod the café. Sit down."

Matt was so astonished at hearing his sister swear, that

he sat down abruptly. Bradford had already parked himself.

"Jack, before Matt came, you said these two had some connection here." Iris' tone was still grating. "You mentioned a woman's name. My mother was Margaret Ann Ellis."

THIRTEEN

Inspector Joe Barnett sat in the interrogation room, drumming his fingers. His own desk was in a corner of a busy working office, and what he needed, for the conversation he was about to have, was privacy.

There was a tap at the door, and a young detective constable looked in.

"You want to see me, inspector?"

He gazed around doubtfully at the bare walls. He must be in for a right rollicking, he decided. But what about? The plain yellow folder in front of the inspector was quietly anonymous.

"Come in George. Sit down."

Barnett opened the folder and began to turn over the familiar report sheets.

"You were one of the officers assigned to interrogating people who left Walt's Café on the night of the Ellis murder," he intoned flatly. "Lorry drivers mostly, who left between the time of the murder, and the time police officers arrived to take charge."

"That's right."

"One of these was a driver named Lewis Riceman. Or so it says here."

The officer screwed up his face.

"Let's see, Riceman. Yes. Yes. He was one of mine. Medium-sized man, clean-shaven, cheeky sort of face. I was able to check his story. No problem. His time was accounted for one hundred per cent. Some other men had their meal with him. Just casual acquaintances. What's the problem, inspector?"

Barnett sighed.

"How old are you, George? Twenty four?"

"Twenty three, sir," replied the mystified George.

"Exactly. And that is the problem."

"Sir?"

The folder closed with a gentle whisper.

"If you'd been thirty three, we wouldn't be sitting here. Your trouble is, and there's nothing you can do about it, you're just not old enough. I dare say you've got a good memory for your villains, eh?"

"Pretty good sir, I like to think."

"But there haven't been so many yet, have there? As you get older, you become a sort of walking filing system. You can remember names, faces, dates, places, an amazing amount of stuff. But you can only remember what you've known. Not things that happened when you were still at school. If you'd been a few years older, you'd have looked at this name, Lewis Riceman. Turned it over in your head. Sort of familiar. But like Reisman. That would be it, you'd think. I wonder if this is Lou Reisman, I've got here. What are you lookng so dumbfounded for?"

"The name, sir. Lou Reisman. I know that all right. One of the big thieves, the Great Bullion Raid, wasn't he?"

"He was George. He was," replied his superior, sadly. "And you had to talk to him, question him, about his presence in the vicinity of a murder case. And I bet he cooperated a treat, didn't he? As soon as he realised you hadn't tumbled to who he was, he was as nice as nine-pence."

The crestfallen officer facing him lowered his eyes.

" Yes. Rather a likeable sort of bloke, I thought. Shocked about the murder. Lovely looking woman like that, he said. What a waste. I can see him now, shaking his head."

Barnett was interested at once.

" Are you sure about that? You're not confusing him with someone else? One of the other people you saw?"

The reply was positive.

" Oh no. That's no mistake. It was this Riceman—sorry, Reisman—all right."

" H'm."

Mrs. Ellis had made a point throughout her married life of never appearing in the café. Did all her work in the background, kept out of sight. In fact, keeping out of sight was something she had been rather good at. As though she had suffered from some kind of phobia about public places. And yet the people of Great Fording were unanimous in their opinion of her as an outgoing, friendly sort of person, anxious to play her part in the community life of that off-the-beaten-track village. But only as far as the parish boundary. She had only ever made one appearance in the main body of the café, if all the evidence was to be believed. Lou Reisman must have been one of the fortunate customers that evening.

In the early days of the Ellis investigation, Joe Barnett had spent a lot of time speculating about the dead woman. A striking-looking girl like that ought not to be cloistered away from the mainstream of life. Ought not to be buried in what was after all a village virtually unchanged since the previous century. He had conjured up his own fancies, to explain the phenomenon. She was a famous ballet dancer, sick of it all, and content to settle for the peace and quiet. She was an escapee from the Iron Curtain agents, or a vital witness against some prominent Mafia boss. Ruby Masters played a dozen roles in the dramas created for her by Inspector Joe Barnett. But that was before the decision was taken against her husband, Walter. All circumstantial, of course, except the gun. That had been found, flung in some bushes a few yards from the house, along with a right-hand glove, to be retrieved and buried later. Both gun and glove were the property of the dead woman's husband, and he had not even attempted to deny that. Even so, it was Barnett's private opinion that the case for the prosecution was thin, and that the likely outcome would be an acquittal.

Now, there was this Reisman development. Barnett was already smarting from the criticism that he'd been lax over the surveillance on the café, in the stolen goods investigation. If anybody should later find that police questioning had been no more than superficial in a murder enquiry involving the same suspect, then his career would be seriously damaged. Any suspect would be bad enough, but a Great Bullion Raider was in a class apart.

The young officer opposite was waiting for him to say something. He pointed a heavy finger across the table.

" Your nice cooperative Mr. Reisman has been nicked, George. Pity you didn't have a nose around his lorry, while you had the chance."

" On what grounds, inspector? I didn't have any right to—"

" An old boss of mine used to say to me, when I was about your age, 'a copper who waits for his rights also waits for his promotions '. You might do well to bear it in mind. Your friend, with the cheeky sort of face, has been spreading stolen goods the length and breadth of the bleeding land. Don't worry George, I'm not going to tell anybody. That's not to say they won't find out anyway. Be a bit more suspicious in future, for your own sake."

The interview was over. The young officer rose, nodded uncertainly, and went out of the room. Barnett frowned. There was still something he didn't like, something that was probably shouting at him, from the closely-typed sheets under his hand. He looked up irritably as a uniformed constable looked in.

"Inspector, there's a man here to see you. And a girl. She's Miss Ellis, daughter of Walter Ellis in the café murder."

"And the man?"

"Stranger. Name of Bradford. Says he used to be at the Yard. He sort of whispered to me, when the girl couldn't hear. Said he'd like to see you alone, first."

"Did he? Did he, now."

Bradford. The private investigator bloke that the Ellis girl had visited in—where was it?—Villiers Street. H'm.

"Right, constable. Let's have a look at Mr. Bradford."

The interrogation room led off the main lobby. Bradford was shown in within seconds. Barnett got to his feet, and they had a look at each other.

Bradford held out his hand.

"I'm Jack Bradford, inspector."

"Joe Barnett," replied the other. Then he cocked his head to one side. "Bradford, John A., President, Small Traders Mutual Trust, Head Office, Villiers Street, London W.1. Formerly Detective Inspector Jabber Bradford, New Scotland Yard, retired on health grounds just over a year ago. Dicky heart. Did I leave anything out?"

Bradford grinned.

"Only my identifying marks. Listen, I'm not without a good opinion of myself, but that famous I'm not. How on earth did you happen to know all that?"

Barnett looked wise.

"Oh, even we country coppers keep our noses to the ground, you know. Have a seat, Mr. Bradford. What can

133

I do for you, that you don't want the girl to know about?"

Each was thinking that the other would be a good man to work with. They were both also reminding themselves that, in the end, their interests would probably conflict. Joe Barnett represented the case against Walter Ellis. Bradford represented Ellis.

"First of all, inspector, let me tell you my official position—"

"Official?"

"Yes. I hadn't one until an hour ago. Now, I represent the interests of the accused, and have been officially appointed by the defence."

"Really? Why should they do that? I mean, no disrespect to you personally, but you're not a lawyer, are you?"

"No, but I have come up with some information. It probably has a bearing on the Ellis case. It's certainly information the police ought to have, and I'm not one of those people who operate outside the law."

"Have a cigarette, Mr. Bradford."

"Thank you."

Bradford held his lighter over the desk, and smoke began to fill the air.

"The daughter hired me in the first place," he began. "She wanted to know if I could find out anything about her step-mother's history. What she was doing before she turned up in Great Fording. That took us back nine or ten years."

He began to recount the story, from the time of his first enquiries in Cockpole Street. When he came to his interview with Jim Tunstall, the inspector's eyebrows shot up.

"Jim Tunstall himself? You actually talked with him?"

"For quite a long time. He was in no doubt that the man Jervis had been killed by Freddie Price."

"Go on."

134

Bradford ground out his cigarette.

" In the old days, before the bullion job, Price and Reisman had an extra partner, Tommy Freeling. He didn't have the stomach for the big one, and when it went wrong, he stopped thieving altogether. No form at all, for the past ten years. I looked him up as well, to chat about old times."

The inspector smiled.

" You must have been a welcome visitor," he remarked. " Stirring up the mud after all those years."

" He wasn't too happy at first," conceded Bradford, " but he told me quite a lot. I wanted any connection there was with Ruby Ellis, or Masters as she was then. Price was quite a ladies' man. It was the old story with Ruby. She'd come to London from the provinces, Price got his hands on her. What she wanted was to break into show business, and he fixed it so that she did. Sort of."

He looked over at his listener. Barnett nodded.

" Put her out on the street, did he?"

" Not quite. He got her into the fringes. The show-girl in the smaller clubs, hostess for visiting businessmen, that kind of stuff. All well paid. But Price kept the money, naturally."

" Naturally."

" Ruby hated the life, and it wasn't long before she began to hate Price as well, but there was nothing she could do, nowhere to go. And of course, she didn't have any cash. It's a very old story."

" Old as the hills. And when Price got nicked for the bullion job, this Ruby took off, and finished up in Great Fording. The dates will fit, no doubt. All right Mr. Bradford, a nice piece of enquiry work, if I may say so. But where does it get us?"

Bradford rested his elbows on the table.

" By itself, not very far. But Tommy Freeling remem-

bered Walt's Café very clearly, from before the time Ruby
went there. I've already said that Price was hot stuff with
the girls. Had his regulars, all over the country. One of
them was Margaret Ann Ellis, the accused man's first wife.
And I believe there was some delay over the inquest, when
she died falling down the stairs. That usually means,
especially to an ex-copper, that the police weren't altogether satisfied."

He leaned back and waited. Inspector Barnett absorbed
this new information.

" Is there any more to tell me?"

" It's possible."

" Ah."

Barnett understood the situation. Bradford wasn't going
to tell him anything else, until he got something in ex-
change.

" You realise I couldn't give you confidential police
information?"

" Absolutely."

" And if you claimed later that I told you anything, I
would deny it absolutely. Might even have you charged?"

" Understood."

" Very well. You are right about the first Mrs. Ellis'
death. The investigating officers were not satisfied at all.
Her injuries were more consistent with her having been
pushed down the stairs, rather than falling by accident.
They fancied the husband for it, mainly because she was
pregnant at the time. Walter Ellis was not the father."

Bradford whistled. This was news indeed.

" But there was nothing that could be pinned on him,"
he muttered. " Nor, presumably, on anybody else."

" That was the situation," confirmed Barnett.

" I see. So when his second wife was murdered, you
naturally looked at him extra hard. I would have done the
same thing. Now then, inspector, with what we've just told

each other, we seem to have a whole new ball game, don't we? It seems reasonable to assume that the man responsible for Mrs. Ellis' condition was Freddie Price. The date of her death was just a few days before the bullion robbery. It looks to me as if our friend Freddie was tidying things up. He intended to leave the country, that's common knowledge. Margaret Ellis may have got wind of it, may even have threatened to blow the whistle on him. It's very convenient that she should have tumbled down the stairs, just at the right time, isn't it?"

"Very. I will admit, Mr. Bradford, that your information intrigues me. The same two women, the same two men. Walter Ellis doesn't seem to have been very lucky, does he? But whatever possessed Ruby to go to the village, in the first place?"

"We can only speculate. She didn't know the country at all. She knew she wanted some God-forsaken spot, where no one from the old life would ever find her. She was often in the company of our three heroes, Price, Reisman and Freeling, when they were on their boozing expeditions. Could have heard Great Fording mentioned, who knows? She wouldn't know anything about Margaret Ellis, that's fairly certain. Freeling was quite clear about one of Price's golden rules. You never tell one woman anything about another woman. You can tell them anything else, about robbery, violence, murder, if you must, and they won't turn a hair. But mention another woman, and you're in trouble."

Barnett snorted.

"Mr. Price isn't all fool then."

"Not a fool at all," agreed the visitor. "Now then, as you will know from the files, there is still fifty thousand pounds from the bullion job unaccounted for. That's point one. Freddie Price was released from prison a few weeks ago. That's point two. Within days of his release, Ruby

Ellis was murdered in the course of a robbery at the café. That's point three, inspector."

The inspector saw a quick objection.

"But Ruby Ellis had buried herself down there. She really was lost to the world. Price has been locked up for years. He would have no way of knowing where to find her. Even if he wanted to."

"That would have been true, until a few weeks ago, when Ruby finally decided to show her face at the café one night. She only did it once, because she was unlucky. There was someone there who recognised her. Someone who was able to pass the word to Price. Ruby stayed away from the place again, after that, but it was too late."

Joe Barnett sucked at a tooth. He was thinking about Lou Reisman, and wondering how much his new ally knew about developments in that direction. He was also tossing up in his mind as to whether he was going to reveal any more.

"It's all speculation, isn't it? And why should Price murder the woman after all these years? You know as well as I do that we can rule out jealousy or revenge, as motives. Those emotions are long dead, after ten years. And even if there is still a flicker, no man with that long a stretch behind him is going to put himself back inside. He'll do a lot to avoid it."

Bradford agreed entirely.

"Spot on. But you didn't mention profit. Fifty thousand pounds is a motive that doesn't die. Suppose Ruby had the money, and took off with it? Price would want it back. That's a solid motive. And I've got another one. Suppose Ruby actually saw Price kill the photographer, Jervis? If that were the case, she could put him back inside any time she chose. You said yourself, any man will do a lot to avoid that. Perhaps Freddie Price decided to kill her, for that very reason."

"H'm. Let's do some more supposing. Suppose you came across this missing cash? You'll be claiming the reward, I imagine? Ten per cent of that lot would be five thousand quid. Not a bad day's work."

"Several days work," corrected the other. "As for the ten per cent, that's just an eye-catcher for the newspapers. By the time they've whittled it down, I'd be lucky to collect two grand."

The inspector's eyes gleamed.

"The way you're going, you may or may not collect it. But I know things you don't know. Seems to me, if there's any talk of a reward, we ought to split it."

Jack Bradford's jaw fell, in his surprise.

"Split it?"

"Half for you, half for the Police Widows and Orphans fund. What do you say?"

That was better. For a moment there—

"I say yes."

"Right. There's a man we ought to talk to. Lou Reisman. He's in custody up North. I'll need clearance. Let's go and find a telephone."

FOURTEEN

Lou Reisman lit a cigarette and stared out of the train window. Most people would have thought it a grey day. The countryside was dull and flat beneath the scudding rain-clouds, but to Lou it looked like the first day of spring. Who could have guessed, a few hours earlier, that he would be here, comfortable and warm on a fast train to London? His lawyer had warned him that although he would request bail as a matter of course, he expected it to be rejected automatically.

"Have the police any ojections?"

The frosty-faced geezer on the bench had even sounded bored as he asked the question. He thought he knew the answer, clever bastard.

"No objections, my lord."

There had been a momentary stillness in the courtroom, as the chief inspector's reply registered. Even the reporters had shaken themselves out of the torpor which was their normal state at hearings of this kind. People looked at each other, for visual confirmation that their ears had not been at fault.

Frosty-face gave a dry cough, which was his way of recovering his composure.

"It seems a little unusual, but if that is the police position, very well."

Very well indeed. Thirty minutes later, Lou was standing outside on the steps of the courthouse, barely listening to what his excited adviser was saying.

"Keep your nose clean, Lou. This is a tremendous break for us."

Us. They always said us. Bleeding Clerk. It was 'us' until somebody had to go down. Then they shoved off.

"Yeah. Right."

"I mean it. They must be worried about something in their case. I'm going straight back to my office, to go through the whole thing again."

The man's glasses were getting steamed up in his enthusiasm.

"I'm going home. First train out."

And here he was. First class compartment, with only one other occupant. Pity he wasn't a bit more sociable. He'd already refused a drink from the new bottle of Haig three times. Ah well. All the more for the rest of us. Since the rest of us only consisted of Lou, he had to keep his conversation to himself, as well as his liquor. Still, his thoughts were happy enough. He didn't need any company really. Just the little paper cup in his hand.

He looked at his newly-returned watch. Another twenty minutes, and they'd be in. He grinned. Wouldn't some people get a surprise. Freddie Price, especially. The news would have been too late for the midday papers, and Lou didn't think this present lark was important enough to be mentioned on the radio news bulletin.

Most of the whisky was gone when they pulled gently to a halt at King's Cross. Lou left the bottle on the seat. Nice surprise for the cleaners. Then he stepped out on to the platform, and joined the busy stream of passengers hurrying for the exit. Silly buggers, rushing about like that. They ought to relax, like him. Just be grateful to be out and around. Free. Let's see. Three o'clock. Freddie and some of the lads would be in a little drinking club they all frequented. A taxi would get him there in twenty minutes. He pushed open the glass doors and went to join the small queue of waiting people.

" It is Lou Reisman, isn't it?"

A tall man stood looking at him enquiringly. Never seen him before.

" Who're you?" he demanded.

" Freddie Price told me to meet you. He's got a welcome-home party. It's all organised. I've got a car round the corner."

" Freddie?"

Good old Freddie. But how would he know? The man waited.

" I don't get it."

Lou sounded petulant, as his mind tried to adjust to this new situation through a haze of fumes.

" It was on the BBC. One o'clock news," explained the

other. ' Surprise release of Great Bullion Raider '. Freddie nearly had a fit. Right, he said. This is a party, no error. Jack, he said, Jack, that's me, get up to the Cross and tell Lou we're going to have a knees up. So here I am."

" One o'clock news, eh?" Lou automatically straightened up, preening himself. " Don't miss much, do they?"

" No," said Jack, almost respectfully. " You're always news, Lou."

" That's right. I was on the box, you know. Twice."

" Yes, I know. I was hoping you'd tell me about it, as we go. Car's just over there."

" Oh, yeah. Sure. Right."

They walked to the car, and Jack opened a rear door. " After you."

Well, normally Lou would have expected to sit in the front. But this bloke must be just a driver, after all. He began to climb into the rear seat. At the same moment, the door on the far side opened and another man got in. " Here."

A final push from behind, and Lou found himself sitting down, wedged between the new arrival and Jack. Then another man materialised, and climbed in behind the wheel. Lou began to feel uneasy.

" What's all this, then? Who are these blokes?"

" It's all right Lou, they're with me," Jack explained, as they drove away. " Told you. It's a party."

Lou huddled back, trying to unscramble his thoughts, and wishing he'd taken it a bit more steady with the booze. Then he noticed something else wrong.

" Here, this isn't the way to the club."

" Not going to the club. Too public," Jack replied. " This is a real private party, this one."

The driver took them expertly through the traffic, then into the emptying streets of dockland, pulling up outside a pair of large wooden doors. Lou watched, fascinated, as he got out of the car, opened the doors, and returned to drive them through. Funny place to have a party.

"Here we go."

The car stopped outside a heavy door. The other began to get out, but Lou held back.

"Come on, my old son, we're here."

Who was he calling his old son? Too bleeding familiar, an unknown talking to a Great Bullion Raider like that. Bet he didn't call Freddie his old son. Might have a bit of fun with this geezer in a few minutes' time.

Reassured by his own ruffled feelings, and the prospect of marking somebody up, Lou got out, swayed slightly, and went through the door. A light was switched on, and he found himself in a narrow wooden passage. The driver was ahead of him, and he now opened another door, motioning Lou inside.

It was a small room. There was no one else there. No people, no booze, no music. Nothing. Just an old bedstead and a few wooden chairs.

"Sit down Lou," commanded Jack.

"'ere, wait a minute. Where's the party, then? Where's Freddie and the others?"

"Sit down."

Hard fingers jammed against his chest, and he sat down with a bump. Fear began to crawl around at the back of his mind.

"Freddie's been delayed," explained Jack.

"So we're the others," added the driver, unsmiling.

"And you're the party," declared the third man.

He looked at their grim, unfriendly faces, one after the other. The taste of the whisky was now sour in his mouth.

"Delayed?" he muttered. "Freddie delayed?"

"Yes. Pity, that was. Had a bit of an accident. He's down at the hospital. London General. No visitors."

Freddie in hospital. That was bad. That was very bad, that was. Surprised at the croaking noise which was suddenly his voice, Lou asked:

"Hospital? What kind of accident?"

"Fell against some nails. Went right through his knee-caps. Terrible it was. I'll show you."

The one who called himself Jack produced a small cardboard box from his pocket, and opened one end. He extracted a three-inch nail, and held it out for Lou to see. One of the other men passed him a hammer. Holding the nail carefully in the middle of one of the chairs, Jack drove it suddenly into the wood. The noise was sickening.

"Like that."

"Must have hurt something terrible," said the driver.

"Shocking," agreed the third man.

"He was in an old warehouse,' Jack explained. "Just like this one, Lou. Anything can happen if a man's not careful, old place like this."

Lou's throat was very dry now, and sweat broke out on his forehead.

"I don't get it," he said hoarsely. "I don't even know you blokes."

Jack nodded.

"Course you don't. I'm forgetting me manners. The name is Masters, Jack Masters. I'm Ruby's little brother."

Oh Gawd, thought Lou, in sudden panic. Ruby never said anything about any brother. Cow.

"Ruby's brother," he repeated dully, half to himself.

"I've been away you see," Jack's tone was almost conversational. "Been out in Aussie the last coupla years. I was very upset when I heard about Ruby. Being her only brother, you see."

"It's very upsetting, that is," nodded the driver.

Lou's mind was still foggy.

"That was a terrible thing to happen," he said. "But

144

Walter Ellis did that. Her husband Walter, he did it."

"No." Jack's voice was flat, impersonal. "He was good to her, good to my sister, that Walter. Besides, he never knew nothing about the money."

"Money?"

Jack struck him suddenly across the face, with the shaft of the hammer. Lou felt dull pain as his cheek split, then warm blood seeped downwards, some into his mouth. He whimpered, and tried to get to his feet. A hard fist slammed into his middle, and he gave a great sigh of agony, collapsing down again.

"We've been waiting for Freddie to be released, you see, Ruby and me." Jack went on talking, as though nothing had happened. "Nothing she could do, while he was inside. Woman on her own, and that. Nothing I could do, either. But we could wait. And we did. As soon as he was out, I started packing up things over in Sydney. Took a few weeks. By the time I got here, Ruby was dead. Of course, the coppers blamed Walter. It's only natural. But they didn't know about the money, either. I was the only one around who did. Well, leaving Freddie out. I was silly there, I must admit. I never thought about you, at all. Never thought you might be waiting for Freddie as well."

Lou's cheek was throbbing with pain now. He was holding a grubby handkerchief against the wound, in a vain effort to staunch the blood.

"I don't know what you're talking about," he pleaded. "What's all this mean? About the money. What money? And me waiting for Freddie. I don't know nothing about it."

They were all mad, he decided. All of 'em. Especially this Jack. And if he'd really done that to Freddie, with the nails, what chance was there of escaping, None at all, he realised hopelessly.

"There was still fifty grand missing from the bullion

job, as you well know. We thought Freddie had it, Ruby and me. Never gave you a thought. Not till Freddie put me onto you. When he had his little accident. Told me how you killed Ruby. Why did you do that, Lou? Did you think she had it?"

Shaking his head desperately, Lou stared into the implacable faces of his tormentors.

"Listen, I never touched her. Never laid a finger on Ruby. And I don't know nothing about any money. Christ, if I had that sort of money, do you think I'd get myself mixed up in a crummy little job worth three hundred quid?"

Jack smiled. It was a bleak, unwarming sight.

"Clever, that was. Freddie explained that. You got yourself caught, on purpose. Practically framed yourself. You'd cop a year, maybe two. By the time you came out, Ruby's murder would be old news. Walter would be doing ten, or perhaps fifteen. Nobody would be interested in little Lou Reisman coming out of stir. You'd collect the money, and disappear. Clever, that was. Even Freddie admitted that."

Frustrated rage and pain fused suddenly together in Lou's tormented mind.

"Lying bastard," he shouted. "Lying bastard. I never touched her. It was Freddie. He done her in himself. It wasn't me. I never even knew he meant to fix her. He never said."

Jack and the others looked at each other.

"Pull the other one, Lou," Jack said softly. "Why would Freddie want to hurt Ruby? He didn't even know where she was."

Lou was in full flight now.

"I told him," he shouted. "I took him there that night, the lousy, lying bastard. He went to the house, while I was in the cafe. I never knew he was going to do it. As God is my judge, I never knew."

146

But there was no change in the expressions of the watching men.

"Balls," decided Jack. "Freddie's a naughty man, we all know that. But he's nobody's mug. He's only just done all that porridge. He wouldn't do that to Ruby, risk going back in. Why should he? She wasn't doing nobody no harm, down there. I've had enough of this. Hold him still."

The driver suddenly clamped strong arms around Lou from behind. The other man bent and gripped his legs. Jack took one of the nails and held it against Lou's left knee. Then he picked up the hammer with his free hand.

"Last chance Lou. Where's the money?"

Lou let out an animal wail, and tears began to course down his face.

"He had to. Ruby was the only one who could put him away. There isn't any money."

The hammer stopped in mid-arc. Jack looked annoyed.

"You're talking puzzles, Lou," he complained. "How could Ruby do him any harm? He's done his bird."

Words tumbled out from the sweating, petrified creature in the chair.

"She was there. She saw him do for the queer. That Jervis. She seen him do that. Witness, you see."

Jack looked at the other men, who shrugged.

"Jervis? Never heard of him. Who's he?"

The beginnings of hope dawned in Lou's tortured mind.

"Photographer," he said quickly. "It was him done the passports for us all, on the warehouse job. Cost a bomb, they did. But he was queer, you see. Stuck on Freddie. Didn't want him to go out of the country. Got a bit sloppy one night, when he'd had a few jars. Begged Freddie not to go and leave him. Then he did a silly thing. He said he'd blow the job. People don't talk like that to Freddie. Not to Freddie Price they don't. It was the night they went to collect the passports. Freddie took the money with him. Ruby was there. There wasn't supposed to be no trouble. But when this Jervis started shouting about telling the law, Freddie fixed him. Ruby saw him do it. She grabbed the case with the money in, and ran out. Freddie thought it was just panic. She wouldn't go far. He never saw Ruby again. Nor the money. It was like she vanished. That's the God's honest truth."

Jack stood in front of him, banging the hammer gently against the palm of his hand.

"This is all new, about this Jervis," he muttered. "Never heard his name before. Not even from Ruby."

"It's the truth, I swear. The law never connected that murder with the bullion raid. It was never solved."

"But the money, Lou. What about the money?"

"Don't know nothing about the fifty grand. The only money I know about is what Ruby nicked that night. Should have been ten thousand in that bag. That was the reason Freddie told me he wanted to go down there. Find out what she did with it. See if there was any chance of picking up a few bob. He never said he was going to—to do what he did."

"Did he find any of it?"

Lou shrugged.

"He said no. But he would, wouldn't he? Told me he got a couple of hundred from the safe. Give me fifty, for me petrol, like."

Jack rested the hammer on a chair, and removed the terrible nail away from Lou's kneecap. A tremendous sense of relief flooded over the seated man.

"What you going to do now? It wasn't me, you see. I never touched her. You got to believe me."

"P'raps. Let's play it back, and see how it sounds."

"Eh?"

The man who'd been driving the car reached under the

bed, and pulled out a black case. He pushed at some buttons in the front. Jack's voice filled the room.

" Sit down, Lou."

Lou listened, appalled, to his voice, as he said:

" 'ere, wait a minute. Where's this party then? Where's Freddie and the others."

He shouted out in sudden, new fear.

" That's a tape recording. What's the game?"

" You're very quick today, Lou," smiled Jack, as the other man switched off the machine. " That's a little present, for a friend of mine at the Yard."

Lou was beginning to think more clearly, now that his personal danger was put to one side.

" The Yard? You can't pull that one. Your friend'll hear what you did to Freddie. It's all on there, you know."

" Ah yes," nodded Jack. " But you see, that business about Freddie being in hospital, that was what you might call a sort of fairy story, really. Get you in the mood."

First, the words sank in. Then the implication. Freddie was all right, not been hurt at all. That was a relief. The relief was replaced at once, by the terrible knowledge that he had grassed on Freddie Price, for two murders. In shocked disbelief, Lou muttered:

" He'll kill me. He'll bleeding kill me."

" I should think that's very likely," agreed Jack, cheerfully. " Couldn't blame him, really. He'll be very upset when he finds out you've shopped him, Lou. I shouldn't think your life will be worth a packet of fags. Don't think I'd like to be in your shoes. I wouldn't want to know that a killer like Price was out roaming the streets, looking for me. You know what you're going to have to do, don't you? You'll have to get yourself back in custody, quick. Then you'll have to help the police to get Freddie put away. Put away where he can't get at you."

" Grass? Me?'

"Needs must, my old son. Unless you fancy taking your chances when Freddie finds you."

Lou shook his head.

"Why should he want to? He don't know anything about this. Anyway, it won't stand up in court."

It was Jack's turn to shake his head.

"Shouldn't be needed. Freddie's already looking for you, Lou. You see, some rotten sod told Freddie you grassed on him, while the other investigation was on. Up in Manchester. He's out there somewhere, now. You're free to go, if you like."

Lou didn't move.

"I'm finished," he said, dully.

"No need to be. Help the law. They'll take care of him, you needn't worry about that. And who knows? You might even get a bit knocked off your score up in Manchester. They won't drop it altogether, of course. But they might not push quite so hard. Worth thinking about, isn't it?"

Lou's shoulders sagged.

"Haven't got much choice, have I?"

"Not much."

FIFTEEN

Freddie Price was in a good mood after his day at the races. It had been one of those days when all the horses appeared to be on his side, and having picked three winners and two second places, he was almost four hundred pounds to the good. He and a whole crowd of his friends had made a noisy, jolly day of it, and had carried the spirit back with them to continue the festivities in town. With a large cigar in his mouth, he was leaning against the bar, listening to one of Wee Glasgow's dirty stories, when a voice over his shoulder said:

"Hello Freddie."

He turned towards the familiar face of a plain-clothes detective.

"Hello Mr. Harker. Going to have one?"

Freddie had nothing to fear from the police, and it was quite normal for one or other of the local bill to look into the club from time to time.

"Not just now. I'm working. Matter of fact, I'm a bit embarrassed."

"Embarrassed? How d'ya mean?"

Price wasn't very interested, but it never paid to be rude to the law. You could tell by the copper's face the man was uncomfortable.

"There's a woman down at the station. She says you pinched her handbag this afternoon."

"You what?"

Harker repeated what he'd said, then added:

"She's going to make a complaint, if we don't stop her."

The whole group was listening now. Price removed the cigar from his mouth, and stared incredulously at the speaker.

"A handbag? A bleeding handbag? Me? Mr. Harker, you have got to be out of your tiny mind."

Wee Glasgow chimed in.

"What's this, then? Do you mean we're standing here drinking with a dangerous villain, Mr. Harker? A handbag snatcher?"

Someone at the back began to laugh, and soon the whole party had taken it up.

"Save me from the nasty man."

"Mind my purse, Gladys."

Price joined in. The whole thing was too ridiculous to

resist.

"You took a chance, arresting a wicked man like me, all on your own. I would have thought they'd have sent four blokes out, on a big handbag case like this."

"Six," corrected the man beside him.

"With machine guns," added another.

Harker nodded good-humouredly.

"I know, Freddie. But that's what the silly cow is saying. Where were you at half past three?"

"Watching the three thirty at Cheltenham. Sailor's Cake walked home. Seven to four. I was on him."

"You mean you were at the meeting?" pressed the officer.

"We all was. Everybody in here."

Harker looked all round.

"Quite a lot of witnesses," he observed. "Do you think one of them would come down with us, just to clear it up?"

"We'll all come," shouted a slurred voice. "Won't we lads? Be a right giggle, to see their faces down there."

The scene at the station was hilarious. Seventeen exuberant racegoers arrived, to save Freddie Price from the terrible fate of being charged as a handbag-snatcher. The station sergeant was very good-tempered about it all.

"Very well," he said, when some kind of order had been restored. "I think there's enough witnesses to your whereabouts for us to drop the charge."

"Hooray. Three cheers for the sergeant."

"No, no." The sergeant held up his hand. "Thank you all for coming, and would you please leave now. I'll just get you to sign this little statement, Price."

The others began to file out. Freddie Price peered blearily at the half dozen handwritten lines.

"Don't like signing things," he grumbled.

Wee Glasgow took it from him and read it.

"All it says is where you were this afternoon, man. Stand on me, it's harmless."

The others had all left now. Harker and another officer stood close to the desk. Two uniformed constables were at the street door.

"Needn't bother with it, if you don't want to, Freddie. There was just one other little thing, while you're here."

"Oh yeah? What might that be?"

Wee Glasgow was already at the door, waiting to leave. Freddie Price realised he was alone now. Alone with half a dozen policemen at least.

"Murder, Freddie. A question of murder."

*　　　*　　　*

During all the excitement of Freddie Price's arrest, and the establishment of Walter Ellis's innocence, Jack Bradford had kept away from Great Fording. Now, he was in Inspector Barnett's office, drinking tea, prior to making his overdue call on Iris.

The inspector was speaking.

"According to Lou Reisman, some terrible men roughed him up in London. Started knocking nails into his knees."

Bradford looked surprised.

"Tut tut," he said, making two distinct words of it, "there are some awful things going on up there, inspector. You wouldn't believe."

"Not safe on the streets, are we?"

"No. I don't think the police do enough."

They both grinned. Barnett helped himself to extra sugar.

"What do you suppose Ruby did with the ten grand?" he wondered.

Bradford shrugged.

"The money belonging to Jervis? We don't know that she ever had it, do we?"

"It's in Reisman's statement," objected the policeman.

"Ah yes. Reisman's statement," agreed the other. "But he can only say what he's been told, can't he? And who told him? Freddie Price. Lou would wonder about the money, and it wouldn't do for Price to let him think there was ten thousand going spare. Much easier all round if he thought the girl had done a bunk with it."

"H'm. Still, we can't be sure, can we?"

"We'll probably never know, now. But I just can't fit it in with a girl of that type. I mean, settling down in a dump like Great Fording, when she had enough money to take off. Anywhere. South America, anywhere."

"No, I suppose you're right. Jim Tunstall will be disappointed though. About the other fifty thousand, I mean. It would have been nice if this lot had turned that money up as well. Tidied the whole thing up, that would."

Bradford nodded.

"Well, we mustn't be too greedy. Tunstall told me he always reckoned that missing cash was on the Continent somewhere. Other people seem to agree with him. Anyway, he sounded like a dog with two tails when I told him we— or rather, you—had Price nabbed for that Jervis job. Made his day, that did."

The inspector smiled.

"Good. Have you seen the girl lately?"

"My client?" reminded Bradford. "No. Thought I'd keep out of the way till all the tears and everything were finished. I'm going to run over there after I leave you."

"Pretty girl," said Barnett thoughtfully. "Wonder what she'll do, now that's all over?"

"Get back to her studies, I expect. Life goes on."

"Yes. Well thanks for all the help, Jack. I shall have to get on, too. My super wants to see me in half an hour, and it sounds as if he's in one of his moods."

"Good luck with him."

Bradford drove slowly out to the café. Strictly speaking, he realised, there would be no necessity for him to see Iris again, after today's visit. The point was, did he want to? He was still arguing with himself when he parked outside the house.

Iris had been waiting for him, and kept looking out of the window for his arrival. She was in two minds about his visit. On the one hand, she looked forward to seeing Bradford the man. As to the prospect of seeing Bradford the investigator, she wasn't so sure, and the cause of her concern was the money.

After their father's release, she and Matt had left the matter of the book-keeping until he had been able to adjust to the new situation. Then, one evening, they had broached the subject. Matt had explained that the café appeared to be running normally, but the overall profit was lower than it had been for some years. There was no reason, that either of them could identitfy. Walter Ellis had smiled sadly.

"Reason? I can tell you the reason. It was Ruby. She was a marvel, that woman. Could make those books talk, she could. Look, I'm very proud of you, both of you, for the way you've stuck by me these past months. The way you've run the place, even tried to keep the books straight. No father could have asked for more. You've done a marvellous job. As to the money, well, you can't work miracles. Don't forget, Ruby had been doing the money side for years, knew it inside out. You couldn't expect to do that as well as she did, not in this short time. Don't worry about it."

Matt opened his mouth to argue, but Iris warned him off with a quick shake of her head. Later, when they were alone, she said:

"I'm glad you didn't contradict Dad about the profits. It wouldn't have got us anywhere."

"I know that," he agreed readily. "Or, if it did, it might have been somewhere we'd rather not be. Where do you suppose it came from, Icy? There's only two explanations. Either the old man has been on some kind of fiddle, or Ruby was up to something he didn't know about."

Iris put a hand over her brother's.

"I know, Matt. But does it really matter, any more? Ruby is dead, and nothing will bring her back. Dad's life is more or less ruined. Whatever he, or she, or both of them, may have been up to, it doesn't seem very important now, does it? I'd like to drop it."

So they had agreed, and the subject would not be mentioned again. And now, as she watched Jack Bradford climb out of his car, Iris knew that she would have to make a decision before he left. Either she would tell him about the money she had found, and face up to the inevitable enquiries and probing that would follow, or she would keep quiet. If she did that, she would be guilty of something or other, even if it was only duplicity.

They smiled at each other in the doorway. Iris held out her hand, and he held it too long.

"Do come in."

They both started talking at once, laughed, stopped, and began again. Soon the ice had been broken, and they were chatting away like old friends.

"What will you do now?" he queried.

"Do? Well, just pick up where I left off, I imagine. I'll stay here for another week or two, make sure my father is properly settled. But it's no use my staying longer. I can't take Ruby's place, and it wouldn't be right to try. He has to build himself a different kind of life now, without her. There's no point in trying to evade the inevitable."

Good thinking, he reflected.

"I'm sure you're doing the right thing. I'll be sending a bill for my services, of course. Shall I address it to your father, or to you?"

" Me, please. It was my idea. I wish—"

She paused.

" Yes?"

" I wish all my ideas were as good."

Iris dropped her eyes, feeling suddenly awkward. Bradford was elated.

" In a week or two, perhaps I could give you a ring? We could have dinner or something."

" I'd like that."

It was the moment for him to leave. They stood up at the same time. She wondered whether he might want to kiss her, and what her own reaction would be. He smiled down at her, and she half-closed her eyes.

" What will you do about the money?" he asked brusquely.

" Well I—that is—I'm not, I mean, what money?"

But it was no good. He'd caught her completely off guard.

" I think we ought to sit down again, while you tell me about it," he suggested gently.

The relief of being able to talk was enormous. She told him everything, from the time she first discovered the strange case, including the business of the high café profits.

" How much is left?" he asked her.

" Seventeen hundred and sixty pounds," she replied carefully.

" Why didn't you tell the police about it?"

" My father was already in enough trouble. When I saw the money, I thought—well, I thought he'd been up to something crooked. It wasn't the time for me to go making things worse for him. You can understand that, can't you?"

He ignored the question. Just like a man.

" And now? Why haven't you handed it over now? Or do you still think he's a crook?"

Iris's eyes flashed at his bluntness.

"No, I don't," she snapped. "I don't believe he knows anything about it. I think it belonged to Ruby. And I've been doing some sums. The café is making about a hundred pounds a month more than it should, as I told you. Ruby and my father were married nine years ago, but she only became really involved with the books about eighteen months later. If we assume seven years say, that's eighty four months at one hundred a month. Eight thousand four hundred pounds over the years. With what's left, it makes a grand total of just over ten thousand. I'm only guessing, of course, just theorising."

And doing some nice arithmetic, he admitted.

"Any ideas as to how she might get hold of a sum like that?"

Iris shrugged.

"None. I've racked my brains, but I'm not getting any answers."

He nodded sympathetically.

"I think I can help. You read in the papers that Freddie Price is also charged with an old murder? A photographer in London. A homosexual, by the name of Jervis?"

She was puzzled by the apparent change of subject.

"Er yes, I read something."

He handed her a photograph. It was the one she'd found, the one of Ruby as a young girl.

"Look at the photographer's name," he advised.

She did so, and her eyes widened. Bradford nodded again.

"Yes, it's the same chap. Let me tell you the story."

It took him ten minutes, during which her astonishment mounted. When he reached the end, he said:

"So now you have the whole thing. And you know where the money came from. The thing is, what do we do now?"

158

'We', he'd said. Iris caught the implication of that immediately.

"'We'?" she queried, hesitantly.

"Yes, of course 'we'," he replied. "I'm supposed to be on your side, remember?"

"Thank you," she said simply. "Well, we have to find some way to give it back, don't we? Anonymously, if that's possible."

Bradford lit a cigarette. He was so busy thinking that he forgot to offer her one. She found she didn't mind at all.

"Give it back, yes. But to whom? That's the question. Not to Jervis. He's dead. Not to Price, certainly. That money was subscribed by a whole parcel of villains, and the Lord alone knows where they got it."

"The police?" she suggested timidly.

"That would only stir up trouble. Make life unpleasant all round. More interrogation, more suspicion, more reporters. I've got an idea."

"Please."

"You hire me again. Let me see if I can trace any of Ruby's family. Her parents, a sister perhaps."

"You think it's possible, after all these years?"

His face was grave.

"It's possible," he confirmed. "I'm not saying it's likely, but it is possible. Won't do any harm for me to try. The real sufferer in all this has been Ruby, you know. If she left this money, and your father couldn't have it, for obvious reasons, she would probably just as soon have it go to her own flesh and blood. Anyway, it's just an idea."

Iris felt as though a great weight had been taken from her.

"Oh yes, please. Please, Jack. I'd like you to do that."

"All right, I'll give it a try. For a week or two, anyway. After that, well we'll see."

159

She put a hand on his sleeve.

"Perhaps we could talk about it when you take me out to dinner."

As he was driving away, Matt came down the stairs.

"Was that Jack Bradford's car?"

"Yes."

"Oh. What did he want?"

"Nothing really. He wants me to have dinner with him."

Matt snorted.

"Huh. He must be hard up. Well, if you go, take a tip from me."

"What's that?"

"Don't let him take you to that café across the road. The chips are terrible."

They grinned at each other.

It was going to be all right now.